He cradled the bomb against his chest and, in a single swift motion, pulled out the arming pin, twisted the fuse to five seconds, and slammed down hard on the actuator. Then he reached up and switched the MT from *receive* to *send*.

The last soldiers erupted from the screen and there was a growing gap behind them. Into this space and through the screen he threw the bomb.

After that he kept the switch down and tried not to think about what was happening among the men of the invasion army who were waiting before the MT screen on that distant planet.

ONE STEP FROM EARTH

HARRY HARRISON
ONE STEP FROM EARTH

A TOM DOHERTY ASSOCIATES BOOK

ONE STEP FROM EARTH

Copyright © 1970, 1985 by Harry Harrison

A TOR Book

Published by Tom Doherty Associates
8-10 West 36 Street
New York, N.Y. 10018

Cover art by Tom Kidd

First TOR printing: September 1985

ISBN: 0-812-53972-9
CAN. ED.: 0-812-53973-7

Printed in the United States of America

Contents

INTRODUCTION   7

In the Beginning   9
One Step from Earth   28
Pressure   54
No War, or Battle's Sound   80
Wife to the Lord   111
Waiting Place   132
The Life Preservers   149
From Fanaticism, or for Reward   195
Heavy Duty   212
A Tale of the Ending   239

This is the history of the invention that is called the Matter Transmitter. MT for short. It begins at the beginning, where all stories should begin, and continues far into the future, for a million times a million years.

Along the way we dip into the river of time and come up with fragments of this history. These particles, brief encounters, will have to stand for the whole, for the river travels for too long a distance and is too deep for us to ever explore it all. Never mind, there are these most interesting things to see along the way.

Throughout history—and prehistory—mankind's lot has always been affected by man's inventions. With the development of the wheel all the varied forms of transportation began. Just think what the canal did to the English countryside and way of life. Or what the railroad, then the airplane, did to the entire world. Everything has changed; nothing is the same.

Now think of the changes that will be wrought by another form of transportation. The Matter Transmitter. All you have to do is step through the screen and you are on the other side of the world.

Or on the Moon.

Or another planet.

Or the far side of the galaxy.

Here—step through.

➔ IN THE BEGINNING

THERE WAS A LIGHT KNOCK on the compartment door that Adam Ward heard, ignored. He had turned the lights off and now sat by the window of the train, looking out at the snow-covered, star-lit slopes of the Rockies as they moved silently past. A tunnel wall suddenly blotted out the view and he pursed his lips in annoyance, the rattling-roar of the wheels loud in his ears. The sound ended as suddenly as it had begun, the mountains reappeared. The knocking was louder now on the metal door

"Go away," he called out, the irritations of the last weeks harsh in his voice. All of the hurried arrangements, interviews, security clearances, annoyances. "Go away, I don't want any."

"Porter, sir. Got to fix up your bed."

"Come back later."

"Got to do it now, sir."

Annoyed at the interruption Adam shuffled his feet into his slippers and went to the door, unlocked it to send the man away—the bed would be made up when he wanted it—turned the knob.

Took the burst of gas from the spray can full in his face.

He gasped, coughed hoarsely, then fell to the floor.

The big man pushed the door wide, kicked the fallen man's legs out of the way, then slammed it shut as soon as the small man had hurried in behind him. It had taken only a few seconds; they had not been seen.

"You must move quickly," the big man said, squinting at his watch. "This fool was slow in opening the door. There are only four minutes left." He spoke with a note of admonition, as though it were the other's fault.

The small man ignored this and began to undress. Their relationship had been abrasive since they had met, when this operation had first begun. In response to a polite request for the other's name, he had received only gratuitous insult. "In the cell system we do not use names. You may call me Ivan if that pleases you." The tones had been as insulting as the words.

Under the small man's topcoat he wore a boiler suit with a single zipper. He pulled this down and stepped out of the garment, shivering as the cool air touched his skin.

"All of it," Ivan said as he pulled the jacket from the recumbent figure, bumping the man's head cruelly on the floor. "Right down to your sweet white skin."

The small man opened his mouth to protest, but did not speak. Watching instead as Ivan swiftly undressed Adam Ward. Listening to the instructions he had heard too often before.

"You are new to this business. Therefore you must listen, memorize—and obey without thinking. Fingerprints and dental charts have been taken care of. Yours have been substituted. But we have heard that the Yankees have been developing odor recognition, smell patterns not unlike speech patterns. You will wear Ward's hopefully reeking underwear as well as his shirt with stinking armpits just in case they want to try this little device on you."

"How tastefully you express it." He spoke, despite his determination not to.

"You are too delicate for this rough business. But better a brittle tool than no tool at all. Dress—quickly!"

He pulled on the other's still-warm clothing, disguising his feelings of revulsion, knowing any reaction would only please Ivan. As he was knotting the tie the big man looked at his watch and waved him to the far side of the compartment. As though on cue there was a sharp rap: Ivan unlocked the door and pulled it wide. The newcomer grunted as he entered, moving sideways to get through the door. Big, no fat, just bulging muscle. He carried a large suitcase effortlessly in one hand and filled the tiny compartment with his presence.

Ivan stepped up onto the seat to make room, snapping his fingers at the small man. "Get up here, you." Then added, almost as an afterthought, "Tell me your name?"

"Ward. Adam Ward."

"Very *good*, Adam." A pat on the head for a good dog. They swayed as the engine braked and slowed. "You, finish your work, we're coming into the station."

The giant newcomer allowed himself one brief look of contempt before he kneeled and opened the suitcase. It was empty. Then he reached out and seized the naked body upon the floor.

"No!" Adam said, the single word slipping out. He had known nothing of this.

"Yes," Ivan said, smiling with pleasure. "You would be surprised how small a human being is— when folded up. Particularly a man who weighs just fifty-four and a half kilos. Just what you weigh. See."

With precise motions and apparent ease—had he done this before?—the bearlike man tucked Ward's chin against his chest and slid the torso into the suitcase. Folded the arms neatly, bent the legs and knees back before slipping them into place as well. Adam had a last glimpse of the naked body, of himself, foetuslike inside the case, before the lid snapped shut.

"Ward—open the door and make sure the corridor is empty."

He obeyed the command without thinking. The platform lights of a small station moved into view when he looked through the corridor windows. The train slowed, then stopped.

"No one."

Rough hands pulled him aside and the bearlike man slipped by, the heavy suitcase held lightly in one hand. Ivan went out behind him, turning briefly for one last command.

"I am in the adjoining compartment—but only to be disturbed in dire emergency. I don't want to ever see you again. You know what must be done."

Adam slammed the door harshly, letting it speak for him—at the same time knowing that the other man could not care in the slightest.

Alone for the first time he felt a great relief. His training was finished, all those boring sessions with the gray little men. The operations on his face, the dieting to get down to exactly fifty-four and a half kilos. All that finished and to be forgotten. He brushed the dusty footprints from the seat, then washed his hands in the tiny sink. Sat down in the same spot where Ward had been sitting not five minutes earlier. There was a distant whistle and a clanking as the train started forward. Snow was starting to fall again. He had a brief glimpse of a dark figure putting a large suitcase into a car, then the buildings cut off the sight.

He jumped when there was a knock on the door.

"Porter, sir, come to do up your bed."

Now the real work would begin.

"I assume that you know the very important reason why you have been brought here?" Bhatta-charya asked. His twisted body rested at an odd angle in the wheelchair, his hands clawlike with ancient scars. Adam put aside any natural feelings of compassion and spoke the way Ward himself would have spoken.

"You assume, incorrectly, Professor Bhatta-charya. I was bullied by Federal agents until I agreed to come to this place, my students will take their examinations soon, my own research . . ." He broke off as the fire-scarred hand rose in gentle admonition.

"I am very sorry for any inconvenience. But I assure you that the research you will so ably assist us with here will far surpass your wildest dream." His English was slightly accented, very old-fashioned. "You have met Dr. Levy already I believe. If you will kindly excuse me he will explain everything about the Epsilon experiments. I bid you welcome to our most interesting project."

Levy busied himself lighting an ancient and sulphurous pipe as the wheelchair whined down the corridor and out of sight. He was bald, skinny, relaxed, his face dominated by a nose of heroic proportions. He was one of the top mathematicians in the country—perhaps the world.

"You call me Hymie, I'll call you Adam, more friendly like. Okay?" Adam sniffed mild disapproval and was ignored. "First off we got some control problems and you may be just the guy we need to help. I read your paper on cmos gate arrays, good stuff. And fast, that's what we need. How many gates do you get into your six inch wafer?"

"About twenty thousand now. We use three levels of interconnects, two metal and one polysilicon, with 600ps minimum gate delays."

"Marvelous." He nodded happily and puffed out a cloud of noxious smoke. "We can use all that operational speed—and more. Let me tell you why. The Epsilon project is one that went wrong— or rather right—by accident. What it started out

to be is no longer relevant. They were hitting
samples with high-energy proton streams, different
samples, more and more power. They got from
alpha to beta and on up to delta with no results.
Epsilon gave them more than they bargained for.
With this experiment they punched a hole into
something or somewhere and no one, not even the
great Professor Bhattacharya, has the foggiest of
what has been done.''

"Are you being facetious, Dr. Levy?"

"Hymie to my friends, Adam. Be a friend. We
are like one big happy family here. And to answer
your question—no I'm not. I'm a very serious
guy. Come along and I'll show you what I'm
talking about."

There must have been six inches of glass between the control room and the experimental laboratory, yet Adam could feel his hair stir as the
electrical charge built up, then discharged with a
most impressive display of sparking activity.

"You could light up Detroit for a week with all
that juice," Hymie said. "I'm glad the government's paying the electrical bill. And what, you
might ask, do we get for all that effort? We get
that." He pointed to the monitor screen where a
spot of light blinked for a second then vanished,
the sort of spark you see when your television set
is turned off. "Not too impressive. But let me
amplify the picture and slow it down."

This time the screen showed a jagged metal hole
with what resembled a pool of mercury at the
bottom.

"Plenty of magnification. The biggest one of
these we've done so far has been less than two

millimeters wide and lasted all of five hundred milliseconds. That's when we made the temperature experiment. It worked too—though not in the way that we had expected.'' He searched through the video cassettes scattered on the table, found the right one and inserted it into the machine. ''Very clear picture, very slowed down.''

There were the rough metal walls again, the shining pool at the bottom. Suddenly a thick rod came into view, sliding down toward the surface. It came close, moving toward its mirrored image until they touched, kept moving downwards for an appreciable length of time. Then it stopped and withdrew—to show a truncated end. Most of the rod was missing.

''Melted—or burnt off,'' Adam said.

''Neither. No temperature rise. If anything a brief lowering of the temperature. No metallic particles emitted. It just went in—and never came out. And before you ask, it didn't come out the other side because, and I find this utterly fascinating, the silvery surface has no other side. Can you imagine a substance with only a single surface? It's like trying to think of the sound of one hand clapping.''

The next morning Adam Ward arrived at the lab promptly at nine and quickly found himself immersed in the work. In another life—under another name that he never permitted himself to think about—he had done related research. Not on this scale, not with this sort of funding, but work that had been closely related to the control circuitry he was helping to design now. He had done this until his Country had Called—or rather the heavy-set men, the dark coats, who had shown him why he had no choice but to help. All this was forgotten as he worked with the others to discover the secret of that silvery entity.

When his alarm watch pinged he at first could not remember why it had been set. The letters on the face of the watch simply read MESSAGE. Message? From whom? No, not from anyone but to someone; his spirits sank with the memory. He was now Adam Ward. But he was someone else as well—and the message was a grim reminder of that. It was time to report to those across the Atlantic who had sent him here. He was not at his best for the remainder of the day and left early, blaming a headache. In the security of his room he took out his programmable calculator and shook out the handful of magnetized strips that were various programs and formulae that he used; he found the one with the encoding program. He slowly typed his report into the calculator's memory, ran it through the encoding program then recorded it on another magnetic strip. Without the code it was just electronic hash. He went to bed troubled, but slept well, as he always did.

After work the next day he followed the routine that he had established on the previous three Fridays. He drove first to the car wash, paid, then watched until he saw the government Plymouth dragged into the watery tunnel. Then he crossed the road to Mom's Bar and Grill for a glass of beer. The bar was not what might be called exclusive; at least the beer was cold. He finished the glass quickly, as he always did, then went to the grimy toilet and locked the door behind him. It took only a few seconds to fix the tiny magnetic strip to one end of the bandaid, to reach up and stick it behind the cistern with the other adhesive end. He flushed, unlocked the door and went out. He showed no curiosity about the others in the bar, made no attempt to imagine which of them would retrieve the strip. He crossed back over the road just as they were finished wiping his car dry. It had certainly been easy enough to do. His watch was already set for the date of the next drop. This made it easy for him to put all memory of this from his mind, to think instead about the Epsilon field.

During the next week they worked hard and managed to increase the duration of the field's existence by a factor of ten. Prof. Bhattacharya dropped his bombshell at the weekly report meeting.

"You gentlemen, and lady of course, will I am sure be most interested in a theory about the Epsilon field that Dr. Levy has developed. We have had discussions of an exhaustive and continuous nature and the time has arrived to present you with some of our tentative conclusions. Dr. Levy."

For a change—and a relief—Levy's pipe was not working but lay instead reeking at his elbow. He shook a cautionary finger at Bhattacharya. "In all fairness, I must speak the truth about this discovery. Yes, I did the hack work on the computer to see if the math supported the supposition. But, no, I did not originate the idea. Our illustrious chairman did and all credit where credit is due. Now as to the theory . . ." He took a deep breath and reached for his pipe—pulling his hand back when de Oliveira coughed politely. By mutual consent he had been requested, ordered rather, not to ignite the foul object at these meetings. His fingers twitched and he sighed.

"Now nobody laugh. To put it as simply as I can—the silvery surface that we have been observing is . . . the interface between our plane of existence and another. Or between our dimensions and a space of different dimensions. Or between here and there—only we don't know yet where there is. But we do have an idea how we can find out." There was an expectant silence and he went on.

"We have to construct a second field. In the relationship between the two fields we will find our explanation of this phenomenon."

This was not the end, or even the beginning of the end of the research. But it was the first step along the road to a fuller understanding of the Epsilon phenomenon. While they pursued this line of research Adam saw to it that he had his car washed every Friday, had his single beer at the same time—and had the opportunity to put three more bandaids into place, one month apart. Each time that this had been done he put the matter from his mind until the next time the alarm buzzed. He was as engrossed in the work as anyone else, just as excited as they all were when Bhattacharya elected to sum up what they had discovered and proposed a tentative explanation.

"You have all heard, and appreciated as I have, Dr. Levy's definition and description of Epsilon space. I hope he will excuse me if I attempt to rephrase his excellent work with strictly non-mathematical terms.

"There is another space behind the shining surface, lying in some relationship to our own three-dimensional space. At the present time we do not know the physical dimensions of this other space that we shall call Epsilon space, other than that they cannot be measured in any way by the instruments and techniques that we know. It may be infinitely bigger—or infinitely smaller—or may have no size at all from our point of view. Let us assume this last, for we have seen that if a particle of matter is passed through one screen it will emerge from the other in what appears to be no measurable time at all. We have separated the screens by fifty meters and are still unable to measure any time interval. So let us again assume, for the sake of argument, that there is no measurable time difference in this newly discovered universe. It follows then—and you will permit me this fantastic assumption—that if one screen were here and the other in India, it follows that something that enters one screen would emerge from the other at the same instant. If this be true then the impact of this discovery will certainly change everything, and I am not given to hyperbole as I am sure you all know—this discovery will change everything to do with transportation in our world. Which in turn will change every aspect of the world as we know it. I feel that we have a momentous discovery on our hands."

Levy started to speak—then was struck as silent as the rest. For at that moment they all shared the same vision of humanity and the future. Gone the highways and trains from the face of the Earth, gone the great airliners from the skies, the ships from the sea. All of them gone—replaced by the simple and ubiquitous screens. Step through a screen and you were one step from anywhere else on the planet. The concept was too immense, too staggering to assimilate all at once.

There would be technical problems of course—but the history of mankind's technology had always been the history of refining and improving upon every invention. From the Wright Brothers to Concorde, sailing ships to atomic-powered carriers. The technical problems would be surmounted.

But what kind of a world would it be when all of the problems had been solved?

"I feel a great fear," Levy said. "I see us on the shore of unknown—and deadly—seas and I wish that we could turn back and not begin this voyage into the darkness. But I know that we cannot. But at least we can keep this discovery to ourselves for as long as is needed to do the required research and development in secrecy, keep it from the men of war for as long as we can. Keep it from those countries that will see it as a weapon not an economic blessing."

He continued and others spoke as well, but Adam Ward did not hear them. His thoughts were far away from this place, in a distant country, his native country. Not as rich as this one, with a different system of government. But still his country. He had never been much of a political thinker. Happy only that his masters permitted him to do the work he enjoyed. Happy now, despite all of the difficulties, that they had sent him on this mission. To have been here at this time, to have actually taken part in this work—it was like having been present at the invention of the wheel.

He looked at his watch. Two days to go until the next car wash and beer. It was not his regular Friday to communicate but he had been told that a message could be left in an emergency. The code was a simple one to indicate that he had left a message. Instead of his usual miserly fifteen cent tip he was to leave a dollar bill on the bar.

On Thursday night he stopped at the delicatessen next to his apartment house and bought two sandwiches and a cold six-pack of beer. He had a long evening's work ahead of him and no time for cooking or a restaurant. When he entered the apartment he locked the door carefully behind him and turned on the portable radio as he always did. He carried this with him to the bedroom when he changed his shoes for his slippers, and even took it with him to the kitchen when he opened a beer and put the remaining bottles into the refrigerator. He had built the detector into the radio himself, had tested it often and knew that it was reliable. The apartment had not been bugged in his absence. He had been ordered to take this precaution and did so automatically. His attention was upon the report he had to make and how to compose it so that it would be both detailed and still short. It would be too complex to enter directly, a character at a time, into the hand calculator. He took out his typewriter and slowly and meticulously typed out his notes. It was after nine before he was done, past midnight before he had encoded it all to his satisfaction. After this his neck hurt and he was tired—but he had been trained well. In a large stone ashtray he burned the sheets of paper with his notes and draft—along with the used length of ribbon from the typewriter. He pounded the resultant black mess into dust with a ladle from the kitchen and did not retire until the last fragment had been flushed down the toilet. The work was done and he was satisfied.

He was usually able to put this clandestine part of his life from his mind while he worked, but not this Friday. Up until this moment it had all been part of a game to him. A complex and possibly dangerous game, but one without the importance of the real work that they were doing in the laboratory. But now this had all changed. The armed soldiers at the entrance to the lab, the manifold examinations of his pass, all held a different significance now. They were there to prevent precisely what he was doing. He felt what—pride?—in what he was accomplishing. Perhaps. But he was doing only what he had been trained to do. And until the report had been left his work was not at an end. When five o'clock came he tried not to hurry as he put on his coat and went out to the car.

There must have been an accident somewhere ahead, he could hear the sirens in the distance, while the normally heavy Friday traffic was now stopped dead. He crawled along with the others for five blocks before he could extricate the car and work his way around the jam. The carwash closed at six. If he was late it would be another week before the drop could be made. The thought of waiting for that amount of time was frightening and his hands were damp on the steering wheel and he fought his way through the crawling traffic.

He need not have worried. It was a quarter to six when he pulled into the drive by the pumps, returning the smile of the black man at the till.

"Almost didn't make it," the man said, ringing up the sale. "The wife give you hell with a dirty car for the weekend." Adam Ward nodded and paid—then waited for the light before he crossed the road. They were getting to know him here as well and Mom nodded her well-dyed head and put his beer on the bar before him. He sipped it quickly, suddenly eager to have this matter done with. As he turned to the toilet one of the other customers shuffled in ahead of him and locked the door.

"Sure beat you that time," Mom cackled. "Another beer so you'll really have something to work with!"

He started to say no—then nodded. A second beer might help explain his sudden generosity with the dollar tip.

When he heard the gurgle of the ancient plumbing he gulped the last of the beer, trying not to cough when he did so, and was standing outside when the door rattled open.

"We're just middlemen, Sonny," the old man said, glaring as he emerged from the toilet, and for one heart-stopping moment Adam thought that he had been discovered. But it was the classic remark. "Goes in one end then out the other."

Door locked behind him and tested. Good. Two lengths of magnetic tape this time; there was a lot to report. On tiptoe he reached up and slipped the bandaid into place—and experienced a feeling of intense relief. It was done. His part was finished. Others would process the information he had obtained. Relief, and two beers, gave him good excuse to use the facilities. To flush, to wash his hands in the grimy sink, dry them on his handkerchief then unlock the door. Two grim-faced men stood waiting for him outside.

"You are under arrest," the first man said, showing him a gold badge of some sort. "Just don't make any fuss and you won't get hurt."

Adam was too startled, too numb to react. He let them click the cold handcuffs to each wrist, to pull him firmly toward the front door. There was one glimpse of Mom's hanging jaw, then he was outside and being hustled toward the open door of the waiting limousine. He held back—but was pulled inexorably forward.

"My car," he said. "It's being washed . . ." But when he looked up he saw that a stranger was driving it into the street. His captors said nothing, just pulled him forward and into the back seat. After that a numbness and despair washed over him as they sat in silence during the drive. It was over. All over.

The interrogation took place as soon as they were inside the Federal building. His two captors pushed him into a chair at the large conference table, then sat one to each side of him. They did not remove the handcuffs, perhaps to remind him of his perilous position. A tall man, obviously senior to them, entered and pulled up a chair on the other side of the table, then reached out and turned on the tape recorder.

"What is your name?"

"Adam Ward. What do you think you are doing . . ."

"Answer my questions correctly and don't act stupid. Whoever you are, whatever your name is, we have been watching you since you came here. Who are you—and where is the real Adam Ward?"

"This is preposterous—I want a lawyer . . ."

He went silent as his interrogator slid across very clear photographs of the magnetic bits of tape attached to their bandaids.

"You will talk and you will tell us everything. Now begin."

Adam took a deep breath and let it out with a tremulous sigh. It was over. There was some relief in that. "Take these cuffs off and I'll answer your questions. Isn't this what they call a fair cop in the cinema? In a way I'm glad that it's over. I've done what I had to do. What has been discovered here belongs to all mankind—it is not just the property of one country. If I have done that, why then I have done something important."

"You've done nothing—except probably get yourself shot," the interrogator said with malice-filled satisfaction. "We've monitored all of your drops and know all of the people involved. They'll be picked up tonight. It's all over and you have lost."

"Really," he said, irritated at the man's superior tones, then looked at his watch. "I wouldn't be so sure if I were you. The tapes were just backup. The typed originals are well on their way by now."

The sudden pain drove him to the table, gasping. Then the fist struck his face again, even harder. "Tell us what you mean—tell us!" The pain again. He had meant to keep this part secret until there was time for the contact to be long gone. He had not counted on the pain. He had to speak. It was almost seven. The papers would surely be safe by now.

"What papers?" the interrogator asked. He must have spoken the word aloud, although he had no memory of doing so.

"The notes I typed," he said through puffed lips. "I always typed the report out before encoding it. Then I left the sheets under the mat in the car when I brought it into the carwash. Each time when the car was returned the sheets were gone."

There was a silence and he sat up, shaking. But he had them, he could tell by the grim expressions on their faces. They had not known about the carwash.

"You are out of your mind, you commie bastard," the man who had struck him shouted. "Every guy in that carwash is black. You Russkies are good—but not that good. You don't have any black Russians yet."

"I beg your pardon," Adam said, speaking slowly through his bloodied lips. "Of course those chaps are black. Mostly from the West Indies. Good agents. And I resent the suggestion that I am Russian. I'm Canadian, Oxford graduate, Rutherford Laboratories. I believe my recruiters were MI5. British, you know."

Even though it hurt he found himself smiling at their shocked faces. "Nice of you to share your technical advances with your allies. Greatly appreciated."

➔ ONE STEP FROM EARTH

THIS LANDSCAPE WAS DEAD. It had never lived. It had been born dead when the planets first formed, a planetary stillbirth of boulders, coarse sand, jagged rock. The air was thin and so cold that it was closer to the vacuum of space than to any habitable atmosphere. It was nearly noon and the pallid, tiny disc of the sun was high overhead. Yet the sky was dark, the wan light shining on the uneven plain that was unmarked by any footprint. Silent, lonely, empty.

Only the shadows moved. The sun paced its way slowly across the horizon until it set. Night came and with it an ever greater cold. Silently the dark hours passed as the stars arched by overhead, until on the opposite horizon the sun appeared once again.

Then something changed. High above there was a tiny flicker of movement as the sun glinted from some shining surface. A motion where none had existed ever before. It grew to a spot of light that blossomed explosively into a long tongue of flame. The flame continued, grew even brighter as it came close to the surface as it dropped then hovered. Dust billowed out and the rocks melted and then the flame was gone.

The squat cylinder dropped the last few feet and landed on wide-stretched legs. Shock absorbers took up the impact, giving way, then slowly leveling out the body of the device. It bobbed slightly for a few seconds and was still.

Minutes passed and nothing more happened. The dust had long settled; the molten slag hardened and cracked in the cold.

With sudden, sharp explosions the side of the cylinder blew away and landed on the ground some yards distant. The capsule bobbed slightly in reaction to this but quickly came to rest. In the area uncovered by the discarded plate were a number of small devices. They were ringed about a gray plate two feet in diameter that resembled an obscured porthole.

Nothing else happened for quite a while, as though some hidden internal device were marking time. It reached a decision because, with a distant humming, an antenna began to emerge from its opening. At first it projected straight out from the side of the capsule until a curved section emerged, then it began to slowly rise until it towered into the air. Even as it was erecting itself a compact television camera also appeared, moving jerkily into view on the end of a jointed arm. It hesitantly changed directions until it was above the circular plate and angled down toward it and the patch of ground below. Apparently satisfied it locked into this position.

With a loud *ping* the circular plate changed color and character. It was now a deep black that seemed to shift without moving. A moment later a transparent plastic container emerged from the surface of the plate, dropping forward and hitting the ground, rolling over.

The white rat inside the container was terrified at first, knocked onto its side as the tube struck the ground. The rat rolled onto its feet and scurried about trying to get a grip with its claws on the slippery walls, climbing up then sliding back to the bottom again. In a few moments it settled down, blinking its pink eyes at the gray wastes outside. There was nothing moving, nothing to see. It sat and began to smooth its long whiskers with its paws. The cold had not yet penetrated the thick walls.

The picture on the television screen was very blurred. But considering the fact that it had been broadcast from the surface of Mars to a satellite in orbit, had then been relayed to the Lunar station and from there sent to Earth, it wasn't really a bad picture. Through the interference and the snow the container could be clearly seen, with the rat moving about inside of it.

"Success?" Ben Duncan asked. He was a wiry, compact man with close-cropped hair and tanned, leathery skin. There were networks of wrinkles in the corners of his eyes as though he had squinted a lot in very cold weather, or before a glaring sun.

He had done both. His complexion was in direct contrast to that of the technicians and scientists manning the banks of instruments. Other than the few Negroes and one Puerto Rican, all of them were the fishbelly white of city dwellers.

"It looks good so far," Dr. Thurmond said. His degree was in physics from MIT. He was quite proud of it and insisted on his title being used at all times. "Wave form fine, no attenuation, flat response, the trial subject went through with a one point three on the co-ord which can't be bettered."

"When can we go through?" Ben asked.

"In about an hour, maybe a little more. If biology gives the okay. They'll want to examine this transmission on the first subject, maybe send another one through. If everything is in the green you and Thasler will go through at once while conditions are optimum."

"Yes, of course, shouldn't wait," Otto Thasler said. Then, "Excuse me." He hurried away. A small man who wore thick-rimmed glasses. His hair was sandy and thin and he had a slouch from many hours over a laboratory bench: he looked older than he was. And he was nervous. There was a fine beading of sweat on his face and this was the third time he had gone to the toilet in less than an hour. Dr. Thurmond had noticed it, too.

"Otto is jumpy," he said. "But I don't think he will be any trouble."

"He'll be all right once we get there. It is the waiting that bothers people," Ben Duncan said.

"It doesn't bother you?" Dr. Thurmond was curious, but there was also a thin edge of malice to his words.

"Of course it does. But let's say that I have experience with this waiting part. I've never gone to Mars through a matter transmitter before but I have been in some strange positions."

"I'm sure you have. Professional adventurer or some such." The malice was clear now; the distrust of the man who was used to giving orders toward the man who did not take them.

"Not quite. I'm a geologist and a petrologist. Some of the rare earths you use in this lab come from lodes I found. They are not always in the most accessible places."

"Well that's fine." Dr. Thurmond's flat tone of voice did not reflect his words. "You have had plenty of experience taking care of yourself so you will be able to help Otto Thasler. He's the man in charge, the one who has to do all the work. You will assist him."

"Of course," Ben said and turned and walked away.

They were a clannish bunch and went out of their way to show him that he was an outsider. They would never have hired him if there had been one of their own people who could do the job. Transmatter Ltd. was richer than many governments, stronger than some as well. But they knew the value of the right man in the right job. A matter transmitter engineer for the trip was easy enough to find; just pick a suitable man from the staff and tell him to volunteer. Otto, a lifetime employee, had had very little choice. Who else would take care of him? In this overpopulated world of 1993 there were few frontiers left and even fewer men who knew their way around them.

Ben had been in the Himalayas when the copter had come for him. His prospecting expedition had been canceled, pressure was put on from Transmatter, and a far better contract offered. He had been pressured into signing on, but that did not matter. Transmatter did not realize, and he had never told them, that he would have gone for one-tenth the preposterous salary they had offered —or even for free. These indoor types just could not realize that he *wanted* to make this trip.

There was a door nearby that opened onto a balcony and he went out to look over the city. He tamped tobacco into his pipe but did not light it. There would be no smoking soon and he might as well begin to get used to it. The air was fairly fresh at this height, but the smog and haze closed in below. Mile after mile of buildings and streets stretched to the horizon, jammed, packed, and turbulent with people. It could have been any city on Earth. They were all like this—or worse. He had come out through Calcutta and he still had nightmares about it.

"Mr. Duncan, come quickly, they are waiting for you."

The technician shifted from one foot to the other and wrung his hands worriedly, holding the door open with his foot. Ben smiled at him, in no hurry, then handed over his pipe.

"Hold that until I get back, will you."

The dressers had almost finished with Otto by the time Ben appeared. His own team rushed forward. They pulled off his coverall, then dressed him from the skin out in layer after layer of protective fabrics. Thermal underwear, a skintight silk cover over that, an electrically heated suit next, electric socks. It was done quickly. Dr. Thurmond came in while their outer suits were being closed and looked on approvingly.

"Leave the outer suit seals open until you get into the chamber," he said. "Let's go."

Like a mother hen with a parade of chicks, he led the way across the cluttered transmission room, between the banks of instruments and under the high busbars. The technicians and engineers turned to watch when they passed and there was even one cheer. This was quickly stifled when Dr. Thurmond looked coldly toward the man. Two dispatchers were waiting for them in the pressure chamber. They closed and sealed the door behind Dr. Thurmond and the two heavily garbed men. They were beginning to sweat. Dr. Thurmond pulled on a heavy coat as the cold air was pumped in.

"This is the final countdown," he said. "I'll repeat your instructions just one more time." Ben could have recited them equally well but he remained silent. "We are now lowering the air temperature and pressure until it matches the Martian atmosphere. Readings just taken there show the temperature at twenty degrees below zero Fahrenheit and holding steady. Air pressure is ten millimeters of mercury. We are dropping to that pressure now. There is no measurable amount of oxygen in the air. Masks at all time, that is never to be forgotten. We are breathing almost pure oxygen in this chamber, but you will put on your masks before you leave. . . ." He stopped and yawned and his ears popped, trying to equalize the pressure in his inner ear. "I will now go into the airlock."

He went and finished his lecture from there, watching them through the inset window. Ben ignored the drone of his voice and Otto seemed too paralyzed to listen. A thermostat closed in the battery case in the small of his back and Ben felt the heating elements grow warm inside his suit. The oxygen tank was slung onto his back and his face mask with built-in goggles was buckled into place. He automatically bit onto the oxygen tube and inhaled.

"Ready for the first man," Dr. Thurmond said, his voice squeaky and distant in the thin atmosphere.

For the first time Ben looked at the shining black disc of the matter transmitter set into the far wall. One of the dispatchers tossed a test cube into it as Ben lay face down on the table. While they were rolling the table forward the report came in. Everything in the green.

"Hold it," Ben said, and the table stopped. He turned to look at Otto Thasler who was sitting rigid, facing the opposite wall. Ben could imagine the terrified expression on the hidden face. "Relax, Otto, it's a piece of cake. I'll be waiting for you at the other end. Relax and enjoy it, man, we're making history."

There was no answer, nor had he expected one. The quicker this part was over the better. They had been practicing the maneuver for weeks and he automatically took the position. Right arm straight forward ahead of him, left arm tight at his side. The matter transmitter screen grew like a great dark eye as the table rolled forward, until it was all he could see in front of him.

"Do it," he ordered, and they pushed smoothly against his feet.

Sliding. Hand wrist arm vanishing. Feeling nothing. A moment of recoil, of twisting pain, as his head went through, then he was looking at the coarse pebbles on the ground. He pushed aside the test cube and put his hand flat to break his fall. Then his other arm was through and his legs. Falling sideways in an easy roll his hip struck something hard.

Ben sat up, rubbing the sore spot and looked at the plastic container that he had landed on. Inside was a dead rat, rigid, wide-eyed, and frozen. A nice omen. He turned quickly away and went through the rest of the drill. The microphone was hanging in the same spot as on the mockup and he switched it on.

"Ben Duncan to control. Arrived okay. No problems." He should say more than that on this historical moment but his brain was empty of inspiration. He looked around at the low, dark hills, the crater nearby, the tiny, bright sun. There was nothing that really could be said.

"Send Otto through. Over and out."

He stood, brushing some dust from his side, and looked at the shining plate. Minutes passed before the loudspeaker rasped, the voice so distorted he had to strain for the meaning.

"We read you. Stand by for transmission. Thasler coming through."

Otto's hand appeared even before the voice ended. It took the radio waves nearly four minutes to reach Mars, but the matter transmission was almost instantaneous since it went through Bhattacharya space where time, as it is normally constituted, does not exist. Otto's arm dropped limply and Ben took him by the shoulders, a dead weight that he eased to the ground. Rolling him over Ben saw that his eyes were closed. But he seemed to be breathing regularly. He was probably unconscious. Transmission shock they called it. It wasn't uncommon. He should come to in a few minutes. Ben dragged him to one side and went back to the radio.

"Otto is here. Out cold but he looks okay. Send the junk through."

Then he waited. The wind made a thin whistling noise as it blew against his mask, and he felt the cold of it touching his cheeks even through the insulation. He did not mind: there was something almost reassuring that the wind could blow, the hard ground push against his feet, that the sun still shone. For all the evidence of his senses he could still be on Earth, perhaps on one of the high plateaus in Assam that he had so recently left. Consciously he knew that the sunshine here was half as strong as back on Earth. But he could remember cloudy, misty days with far less sun. Gravity? With all the equipment he was burdened with he was aware of no difference. Rounded, red hills in the distance, thin bluish clouds drifting across the sun. A remote corner of Earth, that's all it was. He could not grip the reality of Mars. If he had crossed space in a ship, taken weeks or months, he would have believed it. But a few minutes before he had been standing on Earth. He scuffed

at the gravel with his boot and saw the second
plastic tube that had been sent through with the
struggling rat inside.

It was cold, freezing to death. It would scratch
pathetically at the containing walls, then huddle up
and shiver. And it had its mouth open, gasping. It
appeared to have an even chance of running out of
air or freezing. Just a laboratory animal; thousands
like it died every day in the cause of science. On
Earth. But this one was here, perhaps the only
other living thing on the planet. Ben knelt and
twisted the lid off the tube.

The end was quicker than he had thought possible. The rat took one breath of the Martian air,
gave a convulsive contraction of its entire body—
and died. Ben had not thought it would be like
that. Of course he had been told on Earth that the
great danger of the Martian atmosphere was its
complete dryness, containing only an unmeasur-
able trace of water vapor. They had said that
inhaling it would scorch the mucous membranes in
the nose, throat, and lungs so fiercely that it would
be the same as breathing concentrated sulphuric
acid. This had seemed a little preposterous. Then.
The rat's staring dark eye filmed as it froze. Ben
straightened up and pushed his face mask tighter
against his face. Then went to check Otto, still
unconscious, to make sure his was correctly in
place, too.

No, this was not Earth. He could believe it now.

"Attention please," the loudspeaker chattered.
"Will you be able to handle equipment yourself?
Is Thasler still unconscious? Loads were estimated
for two-man manipulation. Report."

Ben grabbed the microphone.

"God damn you—send that stuff through! By the time you get this message twelve minutes will have been shot. Send it! If anything gets broken you can send replacements. We're alone here, can you understand that, with just the oxygen we have and nothing else, stuck at the other end of a one-way door a couple of hundred million miles from Earth. Send everything—*now! Send it!*"

Ben paced up and down, hammering his fist into his palm, kicking the test blocks and the rat sarcophagus to one side. The fools! He looked at Otto who seemed to be enjoying his rest. A wonderful beginning. He dragged the man to one side where he wouldn't get stepped on. He came back to the screen just as the end of a canister began to emerge.

"And about time!"

Grabbing the end he ran forward until the other end appeared and clanged to the ground. OXYGEN—FOOD the painted letters on it read. Fine. He kicked it rolling to one side and jumped for the next one.

The demand regulator on his back was clicking regularly, feeding him an almost steady flow of pure oxygen, and his head was swimming with fatigue. The ground all about was littered with containers, tubes, and bundles of all lengths, but all with the same diameter. Otto tapped him on the shoulder and he dropped the case he was dragging.

"I passed out, I'm sorry. Is anything—"

"Shut up and grab that tube that's jamming up in front of the screen."

One, two more, then Ben looked on and blinked as a shining dural plate fell from the screen and clattered to the ground. He bent over and saw that someone had lettered on it with red grease pencil.

"SUGGEST YOU CHECK OXYGEN TANK LEVEL. ERECT SHELTER. CHANGE TANKS."

"Someone is thinking now," Ben muttered and jerked his thumb at the tank on his back. "What does it read?"

"Just a quarter left."

"They're right. Erecting the shelter gets priority."

Otto rooted about among the canisters while Ben stretched out the long and unwieldy fabric sausage. The fastenings snapped open easily and he spread it out flat just as he had done in training. Only during training he had not hovered on the edge of exhaustion. He staggered with fatigue now as he fought the heavy shelter material with clumsy gloves. It was finally done and he looked up to see Otto fastening a tank to an inlet tube with the quick fastening attachment.

"What the hell do you think you are doing?" Ben croaked out the words, rasping in his dry throat. He hit Otto on the shoulder, knocking him sprawling.

Otto just lay there, wide-eyed and silent, as though he thought Ben had gone mad. Shaking with anger Ben pointed to the connection.

"Use your eyes. Stay alert. Or you will kill us both. You were attaching a red pipe to a green tank."

"I'm sorry . . . I didn't notice—"

"Of course you didn't, you stupid slob. But you *have* to here. Red is oxygen, what we breathe and what inflates the shelter. Green is the insulating gas that goes into the double wall. Not poisonous, but just as deadly because we can't breathe it.''

Ben made the connections himself and would not let Otto come near the tent again, even threatening him with the wrench when he came close. One tank of oxygen blew the shelter up to a pudding-shaped mound. The second erected it to a firm dome and the pressure valve on the inlet sealed shut automatically. Ben knew that he was almost out of oxygen, but he could not stop before he finished this. He attached the green tank and left it alone to fill the insulating layer by itself. Now the heater. He was dragging it toward the airlock on the shelter. Letting go he staggered one step, two, then dropped unconscious.

"More soup?'' Otto asked.

"A good idea.'' He sipped the cup empty and passed it over. "I'm sorry about the names I called you. Particularly since you managed to save my life right afterwards.'' Otto looked uncomfortable and bent over the pressure stove.

"That's all right, Ben. I deserved what you called me and more. I must have panicked. I'm not used to this kind of thing the way you are.''

"I've never been to Mars before!''

"You know what I mean. You've been everywhere else. I've been to college and to the job and holidays in the Bahamas. I'm a city boy, a real urban dweller.''

"You did fine when I blacked out.''

"Without you there to back me up I suppose I had to. Your tank was empty and I was sure it was anoxia. I knew the shelter had oxygen in it so I just dragged you in here as quick as I could. I pulled off your mask and you seemed to be breathing okay, but it was cold so I went after the heater, then the food. That was all. I just did what had to be done." His words trickled off into silence and he looked owl-like and frightened again behind his heavy-rimmed glasses.

"But that is all that *had* to be done. All that could be done." Ben leaned forward, hammering the words home. "No one could have done more. It is about time you stopped thinking of yourself as one more city boy and faced the fact that you are one of the only two Martian explorers in the whole solar system."

Otto thought about it and almost straightened up his shoulders. "That is true, isn't it?"

"Don't you forget it. The worst is over. We are safely through that box of tricks, which is always what troubled me, and we are at home on Mars. We have food, water, everything we need for months. All we have to do is take normal precautions and we do our job and go back as heroes. Rich ones."

"We have to set up the transmitter first, but that shouldn't be difficult."

"I'll take your word for it, thanks." Ben took the soup and sipped at it noisily because it was hot. "I have no idea why we even have to build another MT when we have one here. In fact I don't even know how the thing works and no one ever bothered to tell me."

"It's simple enough." Otto relaxed, on familiar ground, eager to explain, forgetting their situation for the moment. Which is just why Ben, who knew a good deal about MT theory, had asked him the question.

"The discovery of Bhattacharya space is what made matter transmission possible. Bhattacharya space—or B-space—is analogous to our three-dimensional continuum but nevertheless lies outside of it. But we can penetrate it. The interesting thing is that wherever we penetrate it, from whatever location in our own universe, we appear to come through in the same place there. So by careful alignment it is possible to have two screens sharing the same portion of B-space. The B-space in effect is allowed to penetrate into our space before each screen so that as far as we are concerned the screens no longer exist in our space-time continuum. Whatever enters one comes out of the other. That is it, simply, of course."

"Simple enough—as long as you leave out the details about how the thing is built. But it doesn't explain why we can't leave Mars in the same manner that we came."

"There are a number of factors involved, but the more important ones are alignment power and physical distance."

"You told me distance doesn't affect the screens."

"It doesn't, directly, but it makes alignment much more difficult. The screen out there, the one that was rocketed here to Mars, has a two-foot working diameter, about the very largest we could send. Almost all of its power goes to holding its existence. The transmitter on Earth reaches out and—it is difficult to describe—latches onto it, holds it in shape, stabilizes it to receive transmission. But the same process won't happen in reverse.''

''What would happen if something were sent back in the other direction?''

''There is no 'other direction.' Anything put into this transmitter would be converted to Y radiation and simply sprayed into Bhattacharya space.''

''Doesn't sound healthy at all. What do you say we recharge our oxygen tanks and move the rest of the stuff in here that we are going to need? Then get some sleep.''

''I'm with you.''

They gathered only the immediate essentials—food, air-scrubbing equipment, and the like—then crawled into their sleeping bags.

The next day they were both feeling much better and finished setting up the camp.

On the third day the first pieces of the big matter transmitter were sent through.

It was a component engineer's nightmare. All the units, whatever their function, had to have been designed to fit through a two-foot hole. A number of compromises had been made. After a good many sleepless nights over the drawing boards it had been finally decided that a diesel-electric generator could not be modified enough to get it through. Some nameless sub-engineer bestowed credit on his superiors by suggesting that enough high-charge batteries could be sent through to activate the big six-foot screen long enough to push the generator through in one piece.

The supporting frame had been set up and they had adapted a routine. Ben, who was in far better shape for the physical work, was doing most of the construction work, while Otto worked in the shelter assembling the electronic components. They helped each other when they had to. Ben finally tightened the last bolt on the steel frame, kicked it affectionately, and cycled through the airlock into the shelter. In the morning they could start wiring in the screen-face elements.

Otto was slumped over the work bench, his face flattened against a printed circuit module, his skin red and flushed. His hand was resting on the hot soldering iron and the air stank with the smell of burnt flesh.

Ben dragged him over to his bunk, feeling the burning heat of his flesh all the while. "Otto," he said, shaking him, but the man was limp. His breathing was heavy and slow and he would not regain consciousness. Ben made a thorough job of bandaging the severely burnt hand while he tried to order his thoughts. He was no doctor, but he had enough field training with medicine to be able to identify familiar diseases and traumatic injuries. This fitted no categories. His mind sheered away from any thoughts of what it really might be. He finally gave Otto a heavy shot of multibiotic and made notes of the man's temperature, respiration, and pulse. Sealing his suit he went to the capsule and called Earth.

"I want this transcribed. I am going to give you some information. Do not answer until I am finished and when I am done do not radio but type copy and send it through the MT. All right. Otto is hurt, sick, something, I'm not sure. These are the details."

He sent what he had observed and what he had

done, then waited the slow minutes until his message was received and the answer had arrived. As he finished reading it he crumpled the paper in anger and grabbed the mike.

"Yes, I have considered the possibility of a Martian disease and no, I will not research and send reports. Get a doctor through at once. Offer enough and you'll get a volunteer. Start sending his equipment now while you are finding and dressing him. *Then* you can send through your microscope and sampling equipment and I will be glad to look for microorganisms in the dirt or wherever you want. As we reported, we found some small plantlike growths, but we didn't bother them. The biologists can look into that. I'll look for your germs for you but only after you have done what I tell you."

His message was understood. Transmatter Ltd. were just as eager as he was to ensure the safety of the expedition; they had a lot of money tied up in it, and were not at all hesitant to risk some more lives in the effort. The doctor, a bewildered young staff medic—who had just signed papers that made his wife financially independent for life—dropped to the ground less than half an hour after the last of his equipment and supplies had arrived. Ben hurried him into the shelter and peeled off his outer clothing.

"I've set up all your stuff on the bench there. Your patient is waiting."

"My name is Joe Parker," the doctor said, but he lowered his extended hand when he saw the look on Ben's face. He hurried over to the sick man. Even after a complete examination he was reluctant to admit the truth.

"It could be an unusual disease—"

"Don't dodge the point. Have you ever seen anything like it before?"

"No, but—"

"That's what I thought."

Ben sat down heavily and poured himself a waterglass of the medicinal brandy, then hesitated and poured a smaller one for the doctor.

"A new disease, something really new? A Martian disease?"

"Probably. That's what it looks like. I'll do everything in my power, Ben, but I have no idea how it will turn out."

They both already knew although they would not admit it out loud. In spite of all the medicines and supportive treatment Otto died two days later. Parker made a postmortem examination and discovered that most of the victim's brain had been destroyed by an unknown organism. He froze samples and made numerous slides while Ben worked on the large transmitter. Word about what had happened must have circulated among the staff on Earth because it took four more days to pressure an engineer into volunteering to finish the technical end of the MT. He was a frightened, silent man named Mart Kennedy and Ben did not question him about his motives because he did not really want to know what kind of measures had been used. The work went quickly then, even though a dark shadow seemed to hang over their lives. They ate together without much conversation and pushed as hard as they could with the construction. Dr.

Parker had been working diligently and thought that he had obtained a transparent liquid that contained the submicroscopic agent responsible for the disease. This was tightly stoppered and sealed in a case for transmission as soon as the screen was operating.

It was dawn, the morning of the day when operating tests were to begin. Mart Kennedy rose early to watch the sunrise. He had barely been aware of his surroundings since he had arrived, working with almost no rest on the big screen. That was all right too; thinking about the Martian crud was avoided that way. It was a misapplied, supposedly funny name that did not conceal the waiting horror. Certain death. Mars, it certainly was something. In his most wayout dreams, reading space fiction as a kid, he had never thought he would ever be here. He yawned and went to put the coffee on, then woke the others. Ben's eyes opened instantly and he nodded, fully awake. Parker wouldn't stir and he shook him by the shoulder—then jerked his hand away in sudden fear.

"Ben," he called out, stammering over the sounds as he did when disturbed. "S-something's wrong here."

"The same, the symptoms are all the same," Ben said, hitting his fist again and again against the side of the bed without realizing it. "He has it all right. We'll give him the shots and get the screen working. There's nothing else we can do."

The big matter transmitter had been ready to go the day before, but they had all been too tired to finish the job. Ben made the sick man as comfortable as he could, giving him the medication that had not worked before, then joined Mart Kennedy.

"Everything tests in the green," Mart said. "Ready to activate whenever you say."

"That is right now. The sooner the better."

"Right."

The screen flickered and darkened, then went black all over. Ben had scrawled *send generator* on a canister lid and he threw it into the screen. It vanished. To Earth—or into radiation in B-space. Nothing happened. Seconds trickled by. The batteries could hold the screen for only about a minute.

Then it appeared. The leading edge of the wheeled platform dropped to the ground, and they pulled hard on the handles. The heavy motor-generator came through and they rolled it aside. Behind them the screen wavered and the field died.

"Hook up the leads while I fire it up," Ben said.

He cracked open the valves on the fuel and oxygen tanks and pressed the starter. It kicked over with the first turn. Prewarmed before it had been sent. As the power built up, the transmitter screen was restored. A container with a frightened rat came through and they returned it at once. There were more tests, more rats, and Ben sent a message through with them about Dr. Parker. The answer came quickly enough.

"WE ARE PULLING YOU ALL OUT," the typed message read. "EQUIPMENT IS TO BE LOCKED ON AUTOMATIC AND WE WILL OPERATE FROM THIS END. THANK YOU FOR YOUR AID. TRANSMISSION WILL BEGIN. SEND DR. PARKER THROUGH FIRST."

Ben scrawled a quick note and sent it.

"What will happen to us?"

"A SEALED QUARANTINE UNIT HAS BEEN ESTAB-
LISHED WITH ENTRANCE ONLY BY MT. YOU WILL BE
CARED FOR. EVERYTHING POSSIBLE WILL BE DONE."

"Let's get Parker," Ben said after he had read
the note.

They dressed the unconscious man. Ben used
sticking tape to make sure that the oxygen tube
could not slip out of his mouth. A stretcher had
been sent through earlier and they rolled him onto
it and strapped him into place.

"Take the front," Ben said and they started
toward the tent's airlock. It was cramped, even
with the stretcher standing on end, but they got
through. Ben took up his end of the stretcher
without a word, without even looking back, and
they went to the large transmitter. It was big enough
for them to all go through together.

The light was stronger than they were used to,
and Ben's legs felt heavier. When he opened his
face mask the air was thick and had unusual smells
in it. They stood in a bare hallway with a transparent wall. At least a hundred men were watching
them from the other side.

"Dr. Thurmond speaking, here are your instructions," a loudspeaker said. "You will—"

"Can you hear me?" Ben broke in.

"Yes. You will wait until—"

"Shut up and listen closely. You now have two
specimens, a sick man and a well one. That's
enough. I'm going back to Mars. If I have to die I
might as well die there." He turned to the plate
but Dr. Thurmond's voice stopped him.

"You cannot. It is forbidden. The screen is turned off. You will do as ordered—"

"No I won't," Ben said loudly, and even smiled a little. "I have taken my last order. Those weeks on Mars helped me understand a little about my life on Earth. I don't like people in crowds, in large, stinking, depressing numbers, eating and reproducing and polluting this earth. It was a fine place before the people spoiled it. I'm going back to the world they haven't spoiled. Yet. With some luck perhaps they never will. I remember a dead rat, he came with me to Mars. A laboratory specimen. And that is all I am now in your eyes and I won't have it. I would far rather be the first Martian."

The crowd parted as Dr. Thurmond came forward and stood looking through the transparent wall at Ben, just inches away. He was angry but he controlled it. He raised the wireless microphone and spoke.

"That is all very nice, but it does not bear on the case to hand. You are an employee and bound by contract and you will do as you are ordered. Your room is number three and you will go—"

"I will go back to Mars." Ben slipped the chrome-steel pinch bar out of his pocket and tapped it against the window. Some of the men shrank back but Dr. Thurmond did not move.

"This is a tool," Ben told them. "I will use it. I will find a door or a crack or a window gasket, I will lever away until I get through to your side. And then all the nice Martian crud germs will come out and eat you. So it is really you, Dr. Thurmond, who has no choice. Or rather a choice of two possibilities. You can kill me or send me back to Mars. Now make up your mind.''

Dr. Thurmond's face was drawn with hatred though his voice was calm as ever.

"I won't mention loyalty to you, Duncan, because you have none. But I will tell you that too much money has been spent to jeopardize things now. You will do as ordered.''

"I will *not!*" Ben said, and swung the pinch bar so hard that a chip flew from the plastic surface. This time even Dr. Thurmond winced away.

"Can't you understand that I don't like it here, that I am not staying here? And that just for once you have found someone whom you cannot order about. I'll be of immense value on Mars—if the crud doesn't knock me over. Use that to convince yourself. But do it quick.''

Another chip cracked off the window as he hit it. Dr. Thurmond did not speak but stood rigid. It wasn't until a third chip dropped to the floor that he turned his back suddenly.

"Activate the transmitter," he ordered, then turned off the microphone. The screen went dark. Ben looked at the shimmering surface, then back at the observers.

"Don't make any mistakes, Dr. Thurmond," Ben said. "I know you can have that screen out of sync and can send me through into B-space as a spurt of radiation. And that will be that. But I sincerely hope that you are not going to be that wasteful. I won't ask you for any sympathy, since I know it would please you immensely to kill me in that fashion. But I must remind you that others have heard this talk we have had and you must

have superiors who will resent the loss of a valu-
able man like myself, manager-to-be of your Martian settlement. Why I'll bet they could fire you
just as fast as you fire your underlings.''

Ben started toward the screen, then looked back
to face the still silent audience.

"I'll do a good job of running things on Mars.
If I live I'll keep on doing the work, so you lose
nothing by it. But if I don't do it I imagine you'll
find other applicants for the job pretty hard to
come by.''

Without waiting for an answer he sealed his face
mask and stepped into the screen.

➔ *PRESSURE*

THE TENSION INSIDE THE SHIP ROSE as the pressure outside increased—and at the same rate. Perhaps it was because Nissim and Aldo had nothing at all to do. They had time to think too much. They would glance at the pressure gauges and then quickly away, reluctantly, despite the best of intentions, repeating this action over and over. Aldo knotted his fingers and was uncomfortably aware of the cold dampness of his skin, while Nissim chain-smoked cigarette after cigarette. Only Stan Brandon—the man with the responsibility—stayed calm and alert. While he studied his instruments he appeared completely relaxed, and when he made an adjustment on the controls there was a certain flair to his actions. For some reason this infuriated the other men, though neither would admit it.

"The pressure gauge has failed!" Nissim gasped,

leaning forward against the restraint of his safety harness. "It reads zero."

"It's supposed to, Doc, built that way," Stan said, smiling. He reached over and flicked a switch. The needle jumped while the scale reading changed. "Only way to measure these kind of pressures. Chunks of metal and crystal in the outer hull, different compressibilities, and they compress to destruction. So we switch to the next one—"

"Yes, yes, I know all that."

Nissim contained his temper and dragged heavily on his cigarette. Of course he had been told about the gauges during the briefings. For an instant there it had just slipped his mind. The needle once more moved in steady pace up the scale. Nissim looked at it, looked away, thought about what was outside this seamless, windowless metal sphere, then, in spite of himself, glanced back at the dial again and felt the dampness on the palms of his hands. Nissim Ben-Haim, leading physicist at the University of Tel-Aviv, had too much imagination.

So did Aldo Gabrielli and he knew it; he wished that he had something to do besides watch and wait. Dark-haired, swarthy, with a magnificent nose, he looked typically Italian and was an eleventh-generation American. His position in electronic engineering was as secure as Nissim's in physics—if not better. He was considered a genius whose work with the scantron amplifier had revolutionized matter transmitter mechanics. He was scared.

The *C. Huygens* fell down through the thickening atmosphere of Saturn. That was the ship's official name, but the men who had assembled her at Saturn One called the vehicle simply "the Ball." Essentially that is just what it was, a solid metal sphere with walls ten meters thick, enclosing the relatively minuscule space in its center. The immense, wedge-shaped sections had been cast in the asteroid belt and sent to the Saturn One satellite station for assembly. There, in high orbit, with the unbelievable beauty of the rings and the great bulk of the planet hanging above them, the Ball had taken shape. Molecular welding had joined the sections into a seamless whole, and, just before the final wedge had been slid into place, the MT screen had been carefully placed inside. When the last piece had been joined to the others the only access to the center of the Ball was through the matter transmitter. Once the welders, with their destroying radiation, were through, the final construction could begin. The specially constructed and immense MT screen had been built under the floor, on which were soon mounted the supplies, atmosphere equipment, and apparatus that made the Ball livable for men. Then the controls were installed, as well as the external tanks and jets that transformed it into an atomic-engined space vessel. This was the ship that would drop down to the surface of Saturn.

Eighty years previously the *C. Huygens* could not have been built; the pressure-compacted alloys had not yet been developed. Forty-two years earlier it could not have been assembled because molecular welding had not been invented. Ten years ago the unpierced hull could not have been used since that was when atomic differentiation had first been made practical. No wires or wave guides weakened the solidity of the metal hull of the Ball. Instead, areas of differentiation passed through the alloy, chemically and physically the same as the metal around them, yet capable of carrying separate electric impulses. Taken in its entirety, the Ball was a tribute to the expanding knowledge of mankind. Taking the three men to the bottom of Saturn's twenty thousand-mile deep atmosphere it was a sealed prison cell.

All of them had been conditioned against claustrophobia, yet still they felt it.

"Come in control, how do you read me?" Stan said into his microphone, then switched to *receive* with a quick movement of his jaw against the switch. There was a few seconds' delay as the recording tape clicked out through the MT screen and the return tape rolled back into his receiver.

"One and three," the speaker hissed, a sibilant edge to all the sounds.

"That's the beginning of the sigma effect," Aldo said, his hands still for the first time. He looked deliberately at the pressure gauge. "A hundred thirty-five thousand atmospheres, that's the usual depth where it begins."

"I want to look at the tape that came through," Nissim said, grinding out his cigarette. He reached for his harness release.

"Don't do that, Doc," Stan said, raising a warning hand. "This has been a smooth drop so far but it's sure to get bumpy soon. You know what the winds must be like in this atmosphere. So far we've been in some kind of jet stream and moving laterally with it. That's not going to last forever.

I'll have them send another tape through your repeater.''

"It will take only a moment," Nissim said, but his hand hesitated on the release.

"You can break your skull quicker than that," Stan said pleasantly, and, as if to verify his words, the immense bulk of the Ball surged violently sideways, tipping as it did so. The two scientists clung to their couches while the pilot righted the ship.

"You're an accurate prophet of doom," Aldo said. "Do you dispense good omens as well?"

"Only on Tuesdays, Doc," Stan answered imperturbably as the pressure gauge died again and he switched to the next transmitter. "Rate of fall steady."

"This is taking an infernally long time," Nissim complained, lighting a cigarette.

"Twenty thousand miles to the bottom, Doc, and we don't want to hit too hard."

"I am well acquainted with the thickness of Saturn's atmosphere," Nissim said angrily. "And could you refrain from calling me 'Doc'? If for no other reason than that you address Doctor Gabrielli in the same way, and a certain confusion results."

"Right you are, Doc." The pilot turned and winked as he heard the physicist's angry gasp. "That was just a joke. We're all in the same boat so we can all be cobbers just like at home. Call me Stan and I'll call you Nissim. And what about you, Doc, going to be Aldo?"

Aldo Gabrielli pretended that he did not hear. The pilot was an infuriating man. "What is that?"

he asked as a continuous, faint vibration began to shake the Ball.

"Hard to tell," the pilot answered, throwing switches rapidly, then examining the results on his screens. "Something out there, clouds maybe, that we're moving through. Varying impacts on the hull."

"Crystalization," Nissim said, looking at the pressure gauge. "The top of the atmosphere is two hundred and ten degrees below zero Fahrenheit, but up there the low vapor pressure prevents freezing. The pressure is much higher now. We must be falling through clouds of methane and ammonia crystals—"

"I've just lost my last radar," Stan said. "Carried away."

"We should have had television pickups; we could see what is out there," Nissim said.

"See what?" Aldo asked. "Hydrogen clouds with frozen crystals in them? They would have been destroyed like the other instruments. The radio altimeter is the only instrument that's essential."

"And it's working fine," Stan announced happily. "Still too high for a reading, but it's in the green. Should be; it's an integral part of the hull."

Nissim sipped from the water tube on the side of his couch. Aldo's mouth was suddenly dry as he saw this and he drank, too. The endless fall continued.

"How long have I been asleep?" Nissim asked, surprised that he had actually dropped off despite the tension.

"Just a few hours," Stan told him. "You seemed to enjoy it. Snored like a water buffalo."

"My wife always says a camel." He looked at his watch. "You've been awake for over seventy-two hours. Don't you feel it?"

"No. I'll catch up later. I've got pills here, and it's not the first time that I've pulled a long watch."

Nissim settled back on the couch and saw that Aldo was muttering figures to himself while he worked out a problem on his calculator. No sensation can be experienced indefinitely, he thought, even fear. We were both bloody frightened up there, but it can't go on forever.

He felt a slight tremble of emotion as he looked at the pressure gauge, but it passed quickly.

"It reads solid," Stan said, "but the height keeps shifting." There were dark smears, like arcs of soot, under his eyes, and he had been on drugs for the last thirty hours.

"It must be liquid ammonia and methane," Nissim said. "Or semiliquid, changing back and forth from gas to liquid. God knows, anything is possible with those pressures outside. Just under a million atmospheres. Unbelievable."

"I believe it," Aldo told him. "Can we move laterally and perhaps find something solid underneath us?"

"I've been doing that for the last hour. We either have to sink into that soup, or hop up again for another drop. I'm not going to try and balance her on her jets, not with the G's we have waiting for us out there."

"Do we have fuel for a hop?"

"Yes, but I want to hold it for a reserve. We're down close to thirty percent."

"I vote to take the plunge," Nissim said. "If there is liquid down there it probably covers the entire surface. With these pressures and the wind I'm sure that any irregularities would be scoured flat in a relatively short geological time."

"I don't agree," Aldo said. "But someone else can investigate that. I vote to drop on the fuel situation alone."

"Three to nothing then, gents. Down we go."

The steady descent continued. The pilot slowed the immense weight of the Ball as they approached the shifting interface, but there was no unusual buffeting when they entered the liquid because the change was so gradual.

"I have a reading now," Stan said, excited for the first time. "It's holding steady at fifteen kilometers. There may be a bottom to all this after all."

The other two men did not talk as the drop continued, fearful of distracting the pilot. Yet this was the easiest part of the voyage. The lower they sank the less the disturbance around them. At one kilometer there was no buffeting or sideways motion in the slightest. They fell slowly as the bottom approached. At five hundred meters Stan turned over the landing to the computer and, hand poised, stood ready to take command should there be difficulties. The engines blasted lightly, cut off, and, with a single grinding thud, they were down. Stan flipped the override and killed the engines.

"That's it," he said, stretching hugely. "We've landed on Saturn. And that calls for a drink." He mumbled a complaint when he discovered that it took most of his strength to push up from the chair.

"Two point six-four gravities," Nissim said, looking at the reading on the delicate quartz spring balance on his board. "It's not going to be easy to work under all these G's."

"What we have to do shouldn't take long," Aldo said. "Let's have that drink. Then Stan can get some sleep while we start on the MT."

"I'll buy that. My job is done and I'm just a spectator until you boys get me home. Here's to us." They raised their glasses with difficulty and drank.

The burden of the more than doubled gravity had been anticipated. Aldo and the pilot changed acceleration couches so that the engineer could face the instrument panels and the MT screen. When the restraining catches were released, Nissim's couch also swung about so that he could reach the screen. Before these preparations were finished Stan had flattened his couch and was soundly asleep. The other two men did not notice: they were now able to start on their part of the mission. Aldo, as the MT specialist, made the preparatory tests while Nissim watched closely.

"All the remotes we sent down developed sigma effect before they had penetrated a fifth of the atmosphere," Aldo said, plugging in the test instruments. "Once the effect was strong enough we lost all control and we have never had an accurate track past the halfway mark. We've just lost contact with them." He checked all the readings twice and left the wave form on the scope when he sank back to rest his tired back and arms.

"The wave looks right," Nissim said.

"It is. So is everything else. Which means that one-half of your theory, at least, is correct."

"Wonderful!" Nissim said, smiling for the first time since they had begun the flight. His fists clenched as he thought of the verbal drubbings he would administer to the other physicists who had been rash enough to disagree with him. "Then the error is not in the transmitter?"

"Absolutely."

"Then let's transmit and see if the signal gets through. The receiver is tuned and waiting."

"*C. Huygens* calling Saturn One, come in. How do you read me?"

They both watched as the transcribed tape clicked into the face of the screen and vanished; then Aldo switched the MT to receive. Nothing happened. He waited sixty seconds and sent the message again—with the same results.

"And there is the proof," Nissim said happily. "Transmitter, perfect. Receiver, perfect—we can count on that. But no signal getting through. Therefore my spatial-distortion factor must be present. Once we correct for that, contact will be reestablished."

"Soon, I hope," Aldo said, slightly depressed, looking up at the curved walls of their cell. "Because until the correction is made we are staying right here, sealed into the heart of this king-sized ball bearing. And even if there were an exit we have no place to go, stuck here at the bottom of an ammonia sea under twenty thousand miles of lethal atmosphere.''

"Relax. Have a drink while I work out the first corrections. Once the theory is correct the engineering is just a matter of hardware.''

"Yeah," Aldo said, leaning back and closing his eyes.

Stan was still exhausted when he woke up; sleep under this heavy gravity was less than satisfactory. He yawned and shifted position, but stretching proved more debilitating than satisfying. When he turned to the others he saw Nissim working concentratedly with his computer while Aldo held a blood-stained handkerchief to his nose.

"Gravity bleeding?" Stan asked. "I better paint it with some adrenalin.''

"Not gravity." Aldo's voice was muffled by the cloth. "That bastard hit me.''

"Right on that big beak," Nissim said, not looking up from his computer. "It was too good a target to miss.''

"What seems to be the trouble?" Stan asked, glancing quickly from one to the other. "Isn't the MT working?''

"No it's not," Aldo said warmly. "And our friend here blames me for that and—''

"The theory is correct, the mechanics of application are wrong.''

"—when I suggested that there might be an error or two in his equations he swung on me in a fit of infantile anger.''

Stan moved in quickly to stop the developing

squabble, his drill field voice drowning out the others.

"Hold on now. Don't both talk at once because I can't understand a thing you're saying. Won't someone please put me into the picture and let me know exactly what's happening?"

"Of course," Nissim said, then waited impatiently until Aldo's complaints had died down. "How much do you know about MT theory?"

"The answer is simple—nothing. I'm a torch jockey and I stick to my trade. Someone builds them, someone fixes them. I fly them. Would you kindly simplify?"

"I'll attempt to." Nissim pursed his lips in thought. "The first thing you must realize is that an MT does not scan and transmit like, say, a television transmitter does. No signal, as we commonly think of signals, is sent. What is done is that the plane of the screen of the transmitter is placed into a state of matter that is not a part of space as we normally know it. The receiving screen is placed in the same condition and tuning is accomplished once they are locked onto the same frequency. In a sense they became part of one another and the distance of the intervening space does not matter. If you step into one you will step out of the other without any awareness of either time or spatial separation. I am explaining very badly."

"You're doing fine, Nissim. What comes next?"

"The fact that spatial distance between transmitter and receiver does not matter, but the condition of that space does—"

"You're beginning to lose me."

"I'll give you a not unrelated example. Light rays travel in a straight line through space, unless interfered with in some physical manner—refraction, reflection, so forth. But—these rays can also be bent when they pass through an intense gravitational field such as that of the sun. We have noticed the same kind of effect in MT, and corrections are always made for the bulk of the Earth or other planetary bodies. Another condition affecting space appears here deep in the frigid soup this planet calls an atmosphere. The incredible pressures affect the very binding energy of the atoms and stresses are produced. These interfere with the MT relationships. Before we can move an object from one MT screen to another down here we must make allowances and corrections for these new interferences. I have worked out the corrections, we must now apply them."

"Very simple the way he explains it," Aldo said distastefully, dabbing at his nose and examining the results on his handkerchief. "But it doesn't work out that way in practice. No signals are getting through. And our friend will not agree with me that we'll have to step up the strength of our output if we're ever going to punch through all that pressurized gunk out there."

"It's quality not quantity," Nissim shouted, and Stan stepped in once again.

"By that do you mean that we're going to have to unlimber the MT monster down under the floor?"

"I damned well do. That's why it was built in in the first place, with adjustable components rather than sealed block units."

"It will take us a month to move everything and

we'll probably kill ourselves trying," Nissim shouted.

"Not that long, I hope," Stan said, sitting up and trying not to groan with the effort. "And the exercise will be good for our muscles."

It took them almost four days to clear away and get up the flooring, and they were over the edge of exhaustion before they had finished. Mechanical preparations had been made with this eventuality in mind; there were ringbolts to suspend the equipment from, and power hoists to lift it, but a certain amount of physical effort was still needed. In the end almost the entire floor area had been cleared and raised, leaving a ledge around the wall, on which their test equipment and couches alone remained. The rest of the floor consisted of MT screen. From the hard comfort of their couches they looked at it.

"A monster," Stan said. "You could drop a landing barge through it."

"It has more than size," Aldo told him, gasping for air. He could hear the hammer of blood in his ears and was sure that his heart had suffered from the strain. "All the circuitry is beefed up, with spare circuits and a hundred times the power-handling capacity it would need anywhere else."

"How do you dig into its guts for adjustments? I can't see anything except the screen?"

"That's deliberate." He pointed into the threaded hole in the armor, from which they had unscrewed a foot-thick plug. "Our operating controls are in there. Before we leave we put the plug back and it seals itself into place. To make adjustments we have to lift up sections of the screen."

"Am I being dense or is it the gravity? I don't understand."

Aldo was patient. "This MT screen is the whole reason for this expedition. Getting the MT to work down here is vital to us—but only secondary to the original research. When we get out the technicians will come through and replace all the circuitry with solid state, block sealed units—then evacuate. The upper section of the interior of the hull will be progressively weakened by automatic drills. This screen will be tuned to another MT in space above the ecliptic. Eventually the weakened Ball will collapse, implode, push right down on top of the screen. The screen will not be harmed because it will transmit all the debris through into space. Then the phasing will be adjusted slowly until transmission stops. At which point we will have access to the bottom of Saturn's sea. The cryogenicists and high-pressure boys are looking forward to that."

Stan nodded but Nissim was looking up at the cluttered dome above, almost open-mouthed, thinking of that imploding mass of metal, the pressure of the poison sea behind it. . . .

"Let's get started," he said quickly, struggling to rise. "Get the screens up and the changes made. It's time we are getting back."

The other men helped with the labor of lifting the screen segments, but only Aldo could make the needed adjustments. He worked intensely, cursing feebly, with the units that the remote handler placed before him. When he was too tired he stopped and closed his eyes so he would not see Nissim's worried glances to him, up at the dome above, then back to him again. Stan served them food and doled out the G drugs and stimulants with a cheerful air. He talked about the varied experiences of space flight, which monologue he enjoyed even if they did not.

Then the job was done, the tests completed and the last segment of screen slid back into place. Aldo reached into the control pit and pressed a switch: the dark surface changed to the familiar shimmer of MT operation.

"Transmitting," he said.

"Here, send this," Stan said, scribbling *How do you read us?* on a piece of paper. He threw it far out into the center of the screen and it sank from sight. "Now receive."

Aldo flipped the switch and the surface of the screen changed. Nothing else happened. For a heartbeat of time they watched, unmoving, not breathing, staring at that barren surface.

Then, with smooth sinuousness, a length of recording tape sprang into existence and, bent by its own weight, curved and began to pile up. Nissim was the nearest and he reached out and grabbed it, reeling it in until the cut end appeared.

"It works!" Stan shouted.

"Partially," Nissim said coldly. "The quality of transmission is sure to be off and finer adjustments will have to be made. But they can analyze at the receiving end and send us specific instructions."

He fed the tape into the player and switched it on. A booming squawking echoed from the metal walls. It could be perceived as the sound of a human voice only with a great effort.

"Finer adjustments," Nissim said with a small smile. The smile vanished instantly as the Ball rocked to one side, then slowly returned to vertical. "Something has pushed us," he gasped.

"Currents perhaps," Aldo said, clutching to his couch as the motion slowly damped, "or maybe solid floes."

"There couldn't be anything . . . living out there?" Nissim said in a hollow voice.

They were silent, all of them, visualizing something incredibly large, dark, alien. Menacing. The thought was a terrible one. It was Aldo who broke the spell.

"Highly unlikely—though it is an idea I don't want to speculate about. There is no way we can tell what is out there so I suggest that we do not think about it. It's past time we got out of here."

They were fighting against the unending fatigue now, but they tried to ignore it. The end was so close and the security of Saturn One station just a step away. Nissim computed the needed adjustments while the other two lifted up the screen sections again and reset the components. It was the worst kind of work to do in the more than doubled gravity. Yet, within a solar day they were getting sound-perfect tapes and the samples of materials they sent back tested out correct to five decimal places. The occasional jarring of the Ball continued and they did their best not to think about the forces that could move its incredibly massive bulk.

"We're ready to being live testing now," Nissim said into the microphone. Aldo watched the tape with these recorded words vanish into the screen

and resisted a strong impulse to hurl himself after
it. Wait. Soon now. He switched to receive.

"I do not think I have ever been in one place for
so long before in my entire life," Nissim said
staring, like the others, at the screen. "Even in
college, in Iceland, I went home to Israel every
night."

"We take the MT screens for granted," Aldo
said. "All the time we were working at Satellite
One on this project I commuted to New York City
after work. We take it for granted until something
like this happens. It's easier for you, Stan."

"Me?" the pilot looked up, raising his eyebrows. "I'm no different. I get to New Zealand
every chance I have." His gaze went back instantly to the empty screen.

"I don't mean that. It's just that you are used to
being alone in a ship, piloting, for longer times.
Maybe that's good training. You don't seem as
. . . well, as bothered by all this as we do."

Nissim nodded silent agreement and Stan barked
a short, hard laugh.

"Don't kid yourself. When you sweat, I sweat.
I've just been trained differently. Panic in my work
and you're dead. Panic in your work and it just
means taking a few extra drinks before dinner to
cool down. You've never had the need to exercise
control so you've never bothered to learn."

"That's just not true," Nissim said. "We're
civilized men, not animals, with will power—"

"Where was it when you popped Aldo on the
beak?"

Nissim grinned wryly. "Score one for your side.
I admit that I can be emotional—but that's an

essential part of the human existence. Yet you personally have—what should I say—perhaps the kind of personality that is not as easily disturbed.''

''Cut me, I bleed. It's training that keeps one from pressing the panic button. Pilots have been like that right back to the year one. I suppose they have personalities that lean that way to begin with, but it's only constant practice that makes the control automatic. Did you ever hear the recordings in the Voices of Space series?''

The other two shook their heads, looking at the still empty screen.

''You should. You can't guess the date that any recording was made to within fifty years. Training for control and clarity is always the same. The best example is the first, the first man in space, Yuri Gagarin. There are plenty of examples of his voice, including the very last. He was flying an atmosphere craft of some sort, and he had trouble. He could have ejected and escaped safely—but he was over a populated area. So he rode the craft in and killed himself. His voice, right up to the very end, sounded just like all of his other recordings.''

''That's unnatural,'' Nissim said. ''He must have been a very different kind of man from the rest of us.''

''You've missed my point completely.''

''Look!'' Aldo said.

They all stopped talking as a guinea pig came up through the screen and dropped back to its surface. Stan picked it up.

''Looks great,'' he said. ''Good fur, fine whiskers, warm. And dead.'' He glanced back and forth at their fatigue-drawn, panicked faces and smiled.

"No need to worry. We don't have to go through this instant corpse-maker yet. More adjustments? Do you want to look at the body or should I send it back for analysis?"

Nissim turned away. "Get rid of it and get a report. One more time should do it."

The physiologists were fast: cause of death functional disability in the neural axon synapses. A common mishap in the first MT's for which there was a known correction. The correction was made, although Aldo passed out during it and they had to revive him with drugs. The constant physical drain was telling on them all.

"I don't know if I could face lifting those segments again," Aldo said, almost in a whisper, and switched to receive.

A guinea pig appeared on the screen, motionless. Then it twitched its nose and turned and wriggled about painfully, looking for some refuge. The cheer was hoarse, weak, but still a cheer.

"Goodby Saturn," Nissim said. "I have had it."

"Agreed," Aldo said, and switched to send.

"Let's first see what the docs say about the beast," Stan said as he dropped the guinea pig back into the screen. They all watched it as it vanished.

"Yes, of course," Nissim spoke the words reluctantly. "A final test."

It was a long time coming and was highly unsatisfactory. They played the tape a second time.

". . . and those are the clinical reports, gentlemen. What it seems to boil down to is that there is a very microscopic slowing of some of the animal's reflexes and nerve transmission speeds. In all truth we cannot be sure that there has been an alteration until more tests are made with controls. We have no recommendations. Whatever actions you take are up to you. There seems to be general agreement that some evidence of disability is present, which appears to have had no overt effect on the animal, but no one here will attempt to guess at its nature until the more detailed tests have been made. These will require a minimum of forty-five hours. . . ."

"I don't think I can live forty-five hours," Nissim said. "My heart. . . ."

Aldo stared at the screen. "I can live that long, but what good will it do? I know I can't lift those segments again. This is the end. There's only one way out."

"Through the screen?" Stan asked. "Not yet. We should wait out the tests. As long as we can."

"If we wait them out we're dead," Nissim insisted. "Aldo is right, even if corrections are given to us we can't go through all that again. This is it."

"No, I don't think so," Stan said, but he shut up when he realized that they were not listening. He was as close to total collapse as they were. "Let's take a vote then; majority decides."

It was a quick 2 to 1.

"Which leaves only one remaining question," Stan said, looking into their exhausted, parchment faces, the mirror images of his own. "Who bells the cat? Goes first." There was an extended silence.

Nissim coughed. "There is one thing clear. Aldo has to stay because he is the only one who can make adjustments if more are needed. Not that he physically could, but he still should be the last to leave.''

Stan nodded agreement, then let his chin drop back onto his chest. ''I'll go along with that; he's out as the guinea pig. You're out, too, Dr. Ben-Haim, because from what I hear you are the bright hope of physics today. They need you. But there are a lot of jet jockeys around. Whenever we go through, I go first.''

Nissim opened his mouth to protest, but could think of nothing to say.

''Right then. Me first as guinea pig. But when? Now? Have we done the best we can with this rig? Are you sure that you can't hold out in case further correction is needed?''

''It's a fact,'' Aldo said hoarsely. ''I'm done for right now.''

''A few hours, a day perhaps. But how could we work at the end of it? This is our last chance.''

''We must be absolutely sure,'' Stan said, looking from one to the other. ''I'm no scientist, and I'm not qualified to judge the engineering involved. So when you say that you have done the absolute best possible with the MT I have to take your word for it. But I know something about fatigue. We can go on a lot longer than you think—''

''No!'' Nissim said.

''Hear me out. We can get more lifting equipment sent through. We can rest for a couple of days before going back on drugs. We can have rewired units sent through so that Aldo won't have to do the work. There are a lot of things that might be done to help.''

"None of those things can help corpses," Aldo said, looking at the bulging arteries in his wrist, throbbing with the pressure needed to force the blood through his body under the multiplied gravity. "The human heart can't work forever under these kind of conditions. There is strain, damage—and then the end."

"You would be surprised just how strong the heart and the entire human organism can be."

"Yours, perhaps," Nissim said. "You're trained and fit and we, let's face it, are overweight and underexercised. And closer to death than we have ever been before. I know that I can't hold on any longer, and if you're not going through—then I'm going myself."

"And how about you, Aldo?" Stan said.

"Nissim is speaking for me, too. If it comes to a choice I'll take my chances with the screen rather than face the impossibility of surviving here. I think the odds on the screen are much better."

"Well then," Stan said, struggling his legs off the couch. "There doesn't seem to be very much more to say. I'll see you boys back in the station. It's been good working with you both and we'll all sure have some stories to tell our kids."

Aldo switched to transmit. Stan crawled to the edge of the screen. Smiling, he waved goodby and fell, rather than stepped out onto its surface, and vanished.

The tape emerged instants later and Aldo's hands shook as he fed it to the player.

". . . yes, there he is, you two help him! Hello, *C. Huygens,* Major Brandon has come through and he looks awful, but I guess you know that, I mean he really looks all right. The doctors are with him now, talking to him . . . just a moment. . . .''

The voice faded to a distant mumble as the speaker put his hand over the microphone, and there was a long wait before he spoke again. When he did his voice was changed.

''. . . I want to tell you . . . it's a little difficult. Perhaps I had better put on Dr. Kreer.'' There was a clatter and a different voice spoke. "Dr. Kreer. We have been examining your pilot. He seems unable to talk, to recognize anyone, although he appears uninjured, no signs of physical trauma. I don't know quite how to say this—but it looks very bad for him. If this is related to the delayed responses in the guinea pig there may be some connection with higher brain function. The major's reflexes test out A-one when allowance is made for fatigue. But the higher capacities—speech, intelligence, they seem to be, well, missing. I therefore order you both not to use the screen until complete tests have been made. And I am afraid I must advise you that there is a good chance that you will have to remain a longer period and make further adjustments. . . .''

The end of the tape clicked through and the player turned itself off. The two men looked at each other, horrified, then turned away when their eyes met.

"He's dead," Nissim said. "Worse than dead. What a terrible accident. Yet he seemed so calm and sure of himself. . . ."

"Gagarin flying his craft into the ground to save some others. What else could he have done? Could we have expected him to panic—like us? We as much as told him to commit suicide.''

"You can't accuse us of that, Aldo!''

"Yes I can. We agreed that he had to go first. And we assured him that we were incapable of improving the operation of the machine in our present physical condition.''

"Well . . . that's true.''

"Is it?'' Nissim looked Aldo squarely in the eyes for the first time. "We are going back to work now, aren't we? We won't go through the MT as it is. So we will work on until we have a good chance of making it—alive.''

Aldo returned his gaze, steadily. "I imagine we can do that. And if it is true now—were we really speaking the truth when we said we would have gone through the screen first?''

"That is a very hard question to answer.''

"Isn't it, though. And the correct answer is going to be very hard to live with. I think that we can truthfully say that we killed Stan Brandon.''

"Not deliberately!''

"No. Which is probably worse. We killed him through our inability to cope with the kind of situation that we had never faced before. He was right. He was the professional and we should have listened to him.''

"Hindsight is wonderful stuff. But we could have used a little more foresight.''

Aldo shook his head. "I can't bear the thought that he died for absolutely no reason.''

"There was a reason, and perhaps he knew it at the time. To bring us back safely. He did everything he could to get us all returned without harm.

But we couldn't be convinced by words. Even if he had stayed we would have done nothing except resent him. I don't think either of us would have had the guts to go through first. We would have just lain here and given up and died."

"Not now we won't," Aldo said, struggling to his feet. "We are going to stick with it until the MT is perfect and we both can get out of this. We owe him at least that much. If his death is going to have any meaning we are both going to have to return safely."

"Yes, we can do it," Nissim agreed, forcing the words through his taut, closed lips. "*Now* we can."

The work began.

➔ *NO WAR,*
OR BATTLE'S SOUND

"COMBATMAN DOM PRIEGO, I shall kill you." Sergeant Toth shouted the words the length of the barracks compartment.

Dom, who was stretched out on his bunk and reading a book, raised startled eyes just as the sergeant snapped his arm down, hurling a gleaming combat knife. Trained reflexes raised the book and the knife thudded into it, penetrating the pages so that the point stopped a scant few inches from Dom's face.

"You stupid Hungarian ape!" Dom shouted. "Do you know what this book cost me? Do you know how old it is?"

"Do you know that you are still alive?" the sergeant answered, a hint of a cold smile wrinkling the corners of his cat's eyes. He stalked down the gangway, like a predatory animal and reached for the handle of the knife.

"No you don't," Dom said, snatching the book away. "You've done enough damage already." He put the book flat on the bunk and worked the knife carefully out of it—then threw it suddenly at the sergeant's foot.

Sergeant Toth shifted his leg just enough so that the knife missed him and struck the plastic deck covering instead. "Temper, Combatman," he said. "You should never lose your temper. That way you make mistakes, get killed." He bent and plucked out the shining blade and held it balanced in his fingertips. As he straightened up there was a rustle as every man in the barracks compartment shifted weight, ready to move, every eye on him. He laughed.

"Now you're expecting it, so it's too easy for you." He slid the knife back into his boot sheath.

"You're a sadistic bowb," Dom said, smoothing down the cut in the book's cover. "Getting a degenerate pleasure out of frightening other people."

"Maybe," Sergeant Toth said, undisturbed. He sat on the bunk across the aisle. "And maybe that's what they call the right man in the right job. And it doesn't matter, anyway. I train you, keep you alert, on the jump. This keeps you alive. You should thank me for being such an excellent sadist."

"You can't sell me with that argument, Sergeant. You're the sort of individual this man wrote about, right here in this book that you did your best to destroy—"

"Not me. You put it in front of the knife. Just like I keep telling you pinkies. Save yourself. That's what counts. Use any trick. You only got one life, make it a long one."

"Right in here—"

"Pictures of girls?"

"No, Sergeant, words. Great words by a man you never heard of, by the name of Wilde."

"Sure. Plugger Wyld, fleet heavyweight champion."

"No, Oscar Fingal O'Flahertie Wills Wilde. No relation to your pug—I hope. Listen to this. He writes, 'As long as war is regarded as wicked, it will always have its fascination. When it is looked upon as vulgar, it will cease to be popular.' "

Sergeant Toth's eyes narrowed in thought. "He makes it sound simple. But it's not that way at all. There are other reasons for war."

"Such as what?"

The sergeant opened his mouth to answer but his voice was drowned in the wave of sound from the scramble alert. The high-pitched hooting blared in every compartment of the spacer and had its instant response. Men moved. Fast.

The ship's crew raced to their action stations; the men who had been asleep just an instant before still blinking awake as they ran. The crew ran and stood, and before the alarm was through sounding the great spaceship was ready.

Not so the combatmen. Until ordered and dispatched they were just cargo. They stood at the ready, a double row of silver-gray uniforms down the center of the barracks compartment. Sergeant Toth was at the wall with his headset plugged into a phone extension there. Listening attentively, nodding at an unheard voice. Every man's eyes were upon him as he spoke agreement, disconnected, and turned slowly to face them. He savored the silent moment, then broke into the widest grin that any of them had ever seen on his normally expressionless face.

"This is it," the sergeant said, and actually rubbed his hands together. "I can tell you now that the Edinburgers were expected, and that our whole fleet is up in force. The scouts have detected them breaking out of jump space and they should be here in about two hours. We're going out to meet them. This, you pinkie combat virgins, is it." A sound like a low growl rose from the assembled men and the sergeant's grin widened.

"That's the right spirit. Show some of it to the enemy." The grin vanished as quickly as it had come. Cold-faced as always he called the ranks to attention.

"Corporal Steres is in sick bay with the fever so we're one NCO short. When that alert sounded we went into combat condition. I may now make temporary field appointments. I do so. Combatman Priego, one pace forward." Dom snapped to attention and stepped out of the rank.

"You're now in charge of the bomb squad. Do the right job and the CO will make it permanent. Corporal Priego, one step back and wait here. The rest of you to the ready room, double time— *march*."

Sergeant Toth stepped aside as the combatmen hurried from the compartment. When the last one had gone he pointed his finger at Dom.

"Just one word. You're as good as any man here. Better than most. You're smart. But you think too much about things that don't matter. Stop thinking and start fighting. Or you'll never get back to that university. Bowb up and if the Edinburgers don't get you I will. You come back as a corporal or you don't come back at all. Understood?"

"Understood." Dom's face was as coldly expressionless as the sergeant's. "I'm as good a combatman as you are, Sergeant. I'll do my job."

"Then do it—now *jump*."

Because of the delay Dom was the last man to be suited up. The others were already doing their pressure checks with the armorers while he was still closing his seals. He did not let it disturb him or make him try to move faster. With slow deliberation he counted off the check list as he sealed and locked.

Once all the pressure checks were in the green, Dom gave the armorers the thumbs-up okay and walked to the air lock. While the door closed behind him and the lock was pumped out he checked all the telltales in his helmet. Oxygen, full. Power pack, full charge. Radio, one and one. Then the last of the air was gone and the inner door opened soundlessly in the vacuum. He entered the armory.

The lights here were dimmer—and soon they would be turned off completely. Dom went to the rack with his equipment and began to buckle on the smaller items. Like all of the others on the bomb squad his suit was lightly armored and he carried only the most essential weapons. The drillger went on his left thigh, just below his fingers, and the gropener in its holster on the outside of his right leg; this was his favorite weapon. The intelligence reports had stated that some of the Edinburgers still used fabric pressure suits, so lightning prods—usually considered obsolete—had been issued. He slung his well to the rear since the chance that he might need it was very slim. All of these murderous devices had been stored in the evacuated and insulated compartment for months so that their temperature approached absolute zero. They were lubrication free and had been designed to operate at this temperature.

A helmet clicked against Dom's, and Wing spoke, his voice carried by the conducting transparent ceramic.

"I'm ready for my bomb, Dom—do you want to sling it? And congratulations. Do I have to call you Corporal now?"

"Wait until we get back and it's official. I take Toth's word for absolutely nothing."

He slipped the first atomic bomb from the shelf, checked the telltales to see that they were all in the green, then slid it into the rack that was an integral part of Wing's suit. "All set, now we can sling mine."

They had just finished when a large man in bulky combat armor came up. Dom would have known him by his size even if he had not read HELMUTZ stenciled on the front of his suit.

"What is it, Helm?" he asked when their helmets touched.

"The sergeant. He said I should report to you, that I'm lifting a bomb on this mission." There was an angry tone behind his words.

"Right. We'll fix you up with a back sling." The big man did not look happy and Dom thought he knew why. "And don't worry about missing

any of the fighting. There'll be enough for everyone.''

"I'm a combatman—"

"We're all combatmen. All working for one
thing—to deliver the bombs. That's your job now.''

Helmutz did not act convinced and stood with
stolid immobility while they rigged the harness
and bomb onto the back of his suit. Before they
were finished their headphones crackled. A stir
went through the company of suited men as a
message came over the command frequency.

"Are you suited and armed? Are you ready for
illumination adjustment?''

"Combatmen suited and armed.'' That was
Sergeant Toth's voice.

"Bomb squad not ready,'' Dom said, and they
hurried to make the last fastenings, aware that the
rest were waiting for them.

"Bomb squad suited and armed.''

"Lights.''

As the command rang out the bulkhead lights
faded out until the darkness was broken only by
the dim red lights in the ceiling above. Until their
eyes became adjusted it was almost impossible to
see. Dom groped his way to one of the benches,
found the oxygen hose with his fingers, and plugged
it into the side of his helmet; this would conserve
his tank oxygen during the wait. Brisk music was
being played over the command circuit now as part
of morale-sustaining. Here in the semidarkness,
suited and armed, the waiting could soon become
nerve-racking. Everything possible was done to
alleviate the pressure. The music faded and a voice
replaced it.

"This is the executive officer speaking. I'm going to try and keep you in the picture as to what is happening up here. The Edinburgers are attacking in fleet strength. Just after they were sighted their ambassador declared that a state of war exists. He asks that Earth surrender at once or risk the consequences. Well, you all know what the answer to that one was. The Edinburgers have invaded and conquered twelve settled planets already and incorporated them into their Greater Celtic Coprosperity Sphere. Now they're getting greedy and going for the big one. Earth itself, the planet their ancestors left a hundred generations ago. In doing this . . . just a moment, I have a battle report here . . . first contact with our scouts."

The officer stopped for a moment, then his voice picked up again.

"Fleet strength, but no larger than we expected and we will be able to handle them. But there is one difference in their tactics and the combat computer is analyzing this now. They were the ones who originated the MT invasion technique, landing a number of cargo craft on a planet, all of them loaded with matter transmitter screens. As you know, the invading forces attack through these screens direct from their planet to the one that is to be conquered. Well they've changed their technique now. This entire fleet is protecting a *single* ship, a Kriger class scout carrier. What this means . . . hold on, here is the readout from the combat computer. 'Only possibility single ship landing area increase MT screen breakthrough,' that's what it says. Which means that there is a good chance that this ship may be packing a *single* large MT screen, bigger than anything ever built before. If this is so—and they get the thing down to the surface— they can fly heavy bombers right through it, fire pre-aimed ICBM's, send through troop carriers, anything. If this happens the invasion will be successful."

Around him, in the red-lit darkness, Dom was aware of the other suited figures who stirred silently as they heard the words.

"*If* this happens." There was a ring of authority now in the executive officer's voice. "The Edinburgers have developed the only way to launch an interplanetary invasion. We have found the way to stop it. You combatmen are the answer. They have now put all their eggs in one basket—and you are going to take that basket to pieces. You can get through where attack ships or missiles could not. We're closing fast now and you will be called to combat stations soon. So—go out there and do your job. The fate of Earth rides with you."

Melodramatic words, Dom thought, yet they were true. Everything, the ships, the concentration of firepower, it all depended on them. The alert alarm cut through his thoughts and he snapped to attention.

"Disconnect oxygen. Fall out when your name is called and proceed to the firing room in the order called. Toth. . . ."

The names were spoken quickly and the combatmen moved out. At the entrance to the firing room a suited man with a red-globed light checked the names on their chests against his roster, a final check that they were in the correct order. Everything moved smoothly, easily, just like a drill.

Because the endless drills had been designed to train them for just this moment. The firing room was familiar, though they had never been there before. Their trainer had been an exact duplicate of it. The combatman ahead of Dom went to port so he moved to starboard. The man preceding him was just climbing into a capsule and Dom waited while the armorer helped him down into it and adjusted the armpit supports. Then it was his turn and Dom slipped into the transparent plastic shell and settled against the seat as he seized the hand-grips. The armorer pulled the supports hard up into his armpits and he nodded when they seated right. A moment later the man was gone and he was alone in the semi-darkness with the dim red glow shining on the top ring of the capsule that was just above his head. There was a sudden shudder and he gripped hard just as the capsule started forward. As it moved it tilted backward until he was lying on his back looking up through the metal rings that banded his plastic shell. His capsule was moved sideways, jerked to a stop, then moved again. Now the gun was visible, a half-dozen capsules ahead of his, and he thought, as he always did during training, how like an ancient quick-firing cannon the gun was—a cannon that fired human beings. Every two seconds the charging mechanism seized a capsule from one of the alternate feed belts, whipped it to the rear of the gun where it instantly vanished into the breech. Then another and another. The one ahead of Dom disappeared and he braced himself—and the mechanism halted.

There was a flicker of fear that something had gone wrong with the complex gun, before he realized that all of the first combatmen had been launched and that the computer was waiting a determined period of time for them to prepare the way for the bomb squad. His squad now, the men he would lead.

Waiting was harder than moving as he looked at the black mouth of the breech. The computer would be ticking away the seconds now, while at the same time tracking the target and keeping the ship aimed to the correct trajectory. Once he was in the gun the magnetic field would seize the rings that banded his capsule. The linear accelerator of the gun would draw him up the evacuated tube that penetrated the entire length of the great ship from stern to bow. Faster and faster the magnetic fields would pull him until he left the mouth of the gun at the correct speed and on the correct trajectory to intercept. . . .

His capsule was whipped up in a tight arc and shoved into the darkness. Even as he gripped tight on the handholds the pressure pads came up and hit him. He could not measure the time—he could not see and he could not breathe as the brutal acceleration pressed down on him. Hard, harder than anything he had ever experienced in training: he had that one thought—then he was out of the gun.

In a single instant he went from acceleration to weightlessness. He gripped hard so he would not float away from the capsule. There was a puff of vapor from the unheard explosions, though he felt them through his feet. The metal rings were blown in half while the upper portion of the capsule shattered and hurled away. Now he was alone, weightless, holding to the grips that were fastened to the rocket unit beneath his feet. He looked about for the space battle that he knew was in progress, and felt a slight disappointment that there was so little to see.

Something burned far off to his right and there was a wavering in the brilliant sparks of the stars as some dark object occulted them and passed on. This was a battle of computers and instruments at great distances. There was very little for the un-aided eye to see. The spaceships were black and swift and—for the most part—thousands of miles away. They were firing homing rockets and prox-imity shells, also just as swift and invisible. He knew that space around him was filled with signal jammers and false signal generators, but could detect none of this. Even the target vessel toward which he was rushing was invisible. For all that his limited senses could tell he was alone in space, motionless, forgotten.

Something shuddered against the soles of his boots and a jet of vapor shot out and vanished from the rocket unit. No, he was neither motion-less nor forgotten. The combat computer was still tracking the target ship and had detected some minute variation from its predicted path. At the same time the computer was following the prog-ress of his trajectory and it made the slight correc-tion for this new data. Corrections must be going out at the same time to all the other combatmen in space, before and behind him. They were small and invisible—doubly invisible now that the metal rings had been shed. There was no more than an eighth of a pound of metal dispersed through the plastics and ceramics of a combatman's equipment. Radar could never pick them out from among all the interference. They should get through.

Jets blasted again and Dom saw that the stars were turning above his head. Touchdown soon; the tiny radar in his rocket unit had detected a mass ahead and had directed that he be turned end for end. Once this was done he knew that the combat computer would cut free and turn control over to the tiny set-down computer that was part of his radar. His rockets blasted, strong now, punching the supports up against him, and he looked down past his feet at the growing dark shape that occulted the stars.

With a roar, loud in the silence, his headphones burst into life.

"Went, went—gone hungry. Went, went—gone hungry."

The silence grew again but, in it, Dom no longer felt alone. The brief message had told him a lot. Firstly, it was Sergeant Toth's voice, there was no mistaking that. Secondly, the mere act of breaking radio silence showed that they had engaged the enemy and that their presence was known. The code was a simple one that would be meaningless to anyone outside their company. Translated it said that fighting was still going on but the advance squads were holding their own. They had captured the center section of the hull—always the best place to rendezvous since it was impossible to tell bow from stern in the darkness—and were holding it awaiting the arrival of the bomb squad. The retrorockets flared hard and long, then the rocket unit crashed hard into the black hull. Dom jumped free and rolled.

As he came out of the roll he saw a suited figure looming above him, clearly outlined by the disc of the sun despite his black nonreflective armor. The top of the helmet was smooth. Even as he realized this Dom was pulling the gropener from its holster.

A cloud of vapor sprang out and the man vanished behind it. Dom was surprised, but he did not hesitate. Handguns, even recoilless ones like this that sent the burnt gas out to the sides, were a hazard in no-G space combat. They were not only difficult to aim but had a recoil that would throw the user back out of position. Or, if the gas was vented sideways, they would blind him for vital moments. And a fraction of a second was all a trained combatman needed.

As the gropener swung free Dom thumbed the jet button lightly. The device was shaped like a short sword, but it had a vibrating saw blade where one sharpened edge should be, with small jets mounted opposite it in place of the opposite edge. The jets drove the device forward, pulling him after it. As soon as it touched the other man's leg he pushed the jets full on. As the vibrating ceramic blade speeded up the force of the jets pressed it into the thin armor. In less than a second it cut its way through and on into the flesh of the leg inside. Dom pressed the reverse jet to pull away as vapor gushed out, condensing to ice particles instantly, and his opponent writhed, clutched at his thigh— then went suddenly limp.

Dom's feet touched the hull and the soles adhered. He realized that the entire action had taken place in the time it took him to straighten out from his roll and stand up. . . .

Don't think, act. Training. As soon as his feet adhered he crouched and turned looking about him. A heavy power ax sliced by just above his head, towing its wielder after it.

Act, don't think. His new opponent was on his left side, away from the gropener, and was already reversing the direction of his ax. A man has two hands. The drillger was on his left thigh. Even as he remembered it he had it in his hand, drill on and hilt-jet flaring. The foot-long, diamond-hard drill spun fiercely—its rotation cancelled by the counterrevolving weight in the hilt—while the jet drove it forward.

Into the Edinburger's midriff, scarcely slowing as it tore a hole in the armor and plunged inside. As his opponent folded Dom thumbed the reverse jet to push the drillger out. The power ax, still with momentum from the last blast of its jet, tore free of the dying man's hand and vanished into space.

There were no other enemies in sight. Dom tilted forward on one toe so that the surface film on the boot sole was switched from adhesive to neutral, then he stepped forward slowly. Walking like this took practice, but he had had that. Ahead were a group of dark figures lying prone on the hull and he took the precaution of raising his hand to touch the horn on the top of his helmet so there would be no mistakes. This identification had been agreed upon just a few days ago and the plastic spikes glued on. The Edinburgers all had smooth-topped helmets.

Dom dived forward between the scattered forms and slid, face down. Before his body could rebound from the hull he switched on his belly-sticker and the surface film there held him flat. Secure for the moment among his own men, he thumbed the side of his helmet to change frequencies. There was now a jumble of noise through most of the frequencies, messages—both theirs and the enemy's—jamming, and false messages being broadcast by recorder units to cover the real exchange of information. There was scarcely any traffic on the bomb squad frequency and he waited for a clear spot. His men would have heard Toth's message so they knew where to gather. Now he could bring them to him.

"Quasar, quasar, quasar," he called, then counted carefully for ten seconds before he switched on the blue bulb on his shoulder. He stood as he did this, let it burn for a single second, then dropped back to the hull before he could draw any fire. His men would be looking for the light and would assemble on it. One by one they began to crawl out of the darkness. He counted them as they appeared. A combatman, without the bulge of a bomb on his back, ran up and dived and slid, so that his helmet touched Dom's.

"How many, Corporal?" Toth's voice asked.

"One still missing but—"

"No buts. We move now. Set your charge and blow as soon as you have cover."

He was gone before Dom could answer. But he was right. They could not afford to wait for one man and risk the entire operation. Unless they moved soon they would be trapped and killed up

here. Individual combats were still going on about
the hull, but it would not be long before the
Edinburgers realized these were just holding actions and that the main force of attackers was
gathered in strength. The bomb squad went swiftly
and skillfully to work laying the ring of shaped
charges.

The rear guards must have been called in because the heavy weapons opened fire suddenly on
all sides. These were .30 calibre high velocity
recoilless machine guns. Before firing the gunners
had traversed the hull, aiming for a grazing fire
that was as close to the surface as possible. The
gun computer remembered this and now fired along
the selected pattern, aiming automatically. This
was needed because as soon as the firing began
clouds of gas jetted out obscuring everything. Sergeant Toth appeared out of the smoke and shouted
as his helmet touched Dom's.

"Haven't you blown it yet?"

"Ready now, get back."

"Make it fast. They're all down or dead now
out there. But they'll throw something heavy into
this smoke soon. Now that they have us pin-
pointed."

The bomb squad drew back, fell flat, and Dom
pressed the igniter. Flames and gas exploded high
while the hull hammered up at them. Through the
smoke rushed up a solid column of air, clouding
and freezing into tiny crystals as it hit the vacuum.
The ship was breeched now and they would keep it
that way, blowing open the sealed compartments
and bulkheads to let out the atmosphere. Dom and
the sergeant wriggled through the smoke together,

to the edge of the wide, gaping hole that had been blasted in the ship's skin.

"Hotside, hotside!" the sergeant shouted, and dived through the opening.

Dom pushed away through the rush of men who were following the sergeant and assembled his squad. He was still one man short. A weapons man with his machine gun on his back hurried by and leaped into the hole, with his ammunition carriers right behind him. The smoke cloud was growing because some of the guns were still firing, acting as a rear guard. It was getting hard to see the opening now. When Dom had estimated that half the men had gone through he led his own squad forward.

They pushed down into a darkened compartment, a storeroom of some kind, and saw a combatman at a hole that had been blown in one wall, acting as a guide.

"Down to the right, hole about one hundred yards from here," he said as soon as Dom's helmet touched his. "We tried to the right first but there's too much resistance. Just holding them there."

Dom led his men in a floating run, the fastest movement possible in a null-G situation. The corridor was empty for the moment, dimly lit by the emergency bulbs. Holes had been blasted in the walls at regular intervals to open the sealed compartments and empty them of air, as well as to destroy wiring and piping. As they passed one of the ragged-edged openings spacesuited men erupted from it.

Dom dived under the thrust of a drillger, swing-

ing his gropener out at the same time. It caught his
attacker in the midriff just as the man's other hand
came up. The Edinburger folded and died and a
sharp pain lanced through Dom's leg. He looked
down at the nipoff that was fastened to his calf and
was slowly severing it.

Nipoff, an outmoded design for use against unarmored suits. It was killing him. The two curved
blades were locked around his leg and the tiny,
geared-down motor was slowly closing them. Once
started the device could not be stopped.

It could be destroyed. Even as he realized this
he swung down his gropener and jammed it against
the nipoff's handle. The pain intensified at the
sideways pressure and he almost blacked out; he
attempted to ignore it. Vapor puffed out around
the blades and he triggered the compression ring
on his thigh that sealed the leg from the rest of his
suit. Then the gropener cut through the casing.
There was a burst of sparks and the motion of the
closing blades stopped.

When Dom looked up the brief battle was over
and the counterattackers were dead. The rear guard
had caught up and pushed over them. Helmutz
must have accounted for more than one of them
himself. He held his power ax high, fingers just
touching the buttons in the haft so that the jets
above the blade spurted alternately to swing the ax
to and fro. There was blood on both blades.

Dom switched on his radio; it was silent on all
bands. The interior communication circuits of the
ship were knocked out here and the metal walls
damped all radio signals.

"Report," he said. "How many did we lose?"

"You're hurt," Wing said bending over him. "Want me to pull that thing off?"

"Leave it. The tips of the blades are almost touching and you'd tear half my leg off. It's frozen in with the blood and I can still get around. Lift me up."

The leg was getting numb now, with the blood supply cut off and the air replaced by vacuum. Which was all for the best. He took the roll count.

"We've lost two men but we still have more than enough bombs for this job. Now let's move."

Sergeant Toth himself was waiting at the next corridor, where another hole had been blasted in the deck. He looked at Dom's leg but said nothing.

"How is it going?" Dom asked.

"Fair. We took some losses. We gave them more. Engineer says we're over the main hold now so we're going straight down. Pushing out men on each level to hold. Get going."

"And you?"

"I'll bring down the rear guard and pull the men from each level as we pass. You see that you have a way out for us when we all get down to you."

"Do that," Dom said as he floated out over the hole, then gave a strong kick with his good leg against the ceiling when he was lined up. He went down smoothly while his squad followed. They passed one deck, two, then three. The openings had been nicely aligned for a straight drop. There was a flare of light and a burst of smoke ahead as another deck was blown through. Helmutz passed Dom, going faster, having pushed off harder with both legs. He was a full deck ahead when he plunged through the next opening, and the burst of high velocity machine-gun fire almost cut him in two. He folded in the middle, dead in the instant, the impact of the bullets driving him sideways and out of sight in the deck below.

Dom thumbed the jets on his gropener and it pulled him aside before he followed the big combatman.

"Bomb squad, disperse," he ordered. "Troops coming through." He switched to the combat frequency and looked up at the ragged column of men dropping down toward him.

"The deck below has been retaken. I am at the last occupied deck."

He waved his hand to indicate who was talking and the stream of men began to jet their weapons and move on by him. "They're below me. The bullets came from this side." The combatmen pushed on without a word.

The metal flooring shook as another opening was blasted somewhere behind him. The continuous string of men moved by. A few seconds later a helmeted figure—with a horned helmet—appeared below and waved the all-clear. The drop continued.

On the bottom deck the men were jammed almost shoulder to shoulder and more were arriving all the time.

"Bomb squad here, give me a report," Dom radioed. A combatman with a mapboard slung at his waist pushed back out of the crowd.

"We reached the cargo hold—it's immense—but we're being pushed back. Just by weight of numbers. The Edinburgers are desperate. They are putting men through the MT screen in light pressure suits. Unarmored, almost unarmed. We kill them easily enough but they have pushed us out bodily. They're coming right from the invasion planet. Even when we kill them the bodies block the way. . . .''

"You the engineer?"

"Yes."

"Whereabouts in the hold is the MT screen?"

"It runs the length of the hold and is back against the far wall."

"Controls?"

"On the left side."

"Can you lead us over or around the hold so we can break in near the screen?"

The engineer took a single long look at charts.

"Yes, around. Through the engine room. We can blast through close to the controls."

"Let's go, then." Dom switched to combat frequency and waved his arm over his head. "All combatmen who can see me—this way. We're going to make a flank attack."

They moved down the long corridor as fast as they could, with the combatmen ranging out ahead of the bomb squad. There were sealed pressure doors at regular intervals, but these were bypassed by blasting through the bulkheads at the side. There was resistance and there were more dead as they advanced. Then a group of men gathered ahead and Dom floated up to the greatly depleted force of combatmen who had forced their way this far. A corporal touched his helmet to Dom's, pointing to a great sealed door at the corridor's end.

"The engine room is behind there. These walls

are thick. Everyone off to one side because we are going to use an octupled charge.''

They dispersed and the bulkheads heaved and buckled when the charge was exploded. Dom, looking toward the corridor, saw a sheet of flame sear by, followed by a column of air that turned instantly to sparkling granules of ice. The engine room had still been pressurized.

There had been no warning and most of the crewmen had not had their helmets sealed. They were violently and suddenly dead. The few survivors were killed quickly when they offered resistance with improvised weapons. Dom scarcely noticed this as he led his bomb squad after the engineer.

''That doorway is not on my charts,'' the engineer said, angrily, as though the spy who had stolen the information were at fault. ''It must have been added after construction.''

''Where does it go to?'' Dom asked.

''The MT hold, no other place is possible.''

Dom thought quickly. ''I'm going to try and get to the MT controls without fighting. I need a volunteer to go with me. If we remove identification and wear Edinburger equipment we should be able to do it.''

''I'll join you,'' the engineer said.

''No, you have a different job. I want a good combatman.''

''Me,'' a man said, pushing through the others. ''Pimenov, best in my squad. Ask anybody.''

''Let's make this fast.''

The disguise was simple. With the identifying spikes knocked off their helmets and enemy equipment slung about them they would pass any casual examination. A handful of grease obscured the names on their chests.

"Stay close behind and come fast when I knock the screen out," Dom told the others, then led the combatman through the door.

There was a narrow passageway between large tanks and another door at the far end. It was made of light metal and not locked, but it would not budge when Dom pushed on it. Pimenov joined him and between them they forced it open a few inches. Through the opening they saw that it was blocked by a press of human bodies, spacesuited men who stirred and struggled but scarcely moved. The two combatmen pushed harder and a sudden movement of the mob released the pressure and Dom fell forward, his helmet banging into that of the nearest man.

"What the devil you about?" the man said, twisting his head to look at Dom.

"More of them down there," Dom said, trying to roll his R's the way the Edinburgers did.

"You're not one of us!" the man said and struggled to bring his weapon up.

Dom could not risk a fight here—yet the man had to be silenced. He could just reach the lightning prod and he jerked it from its clip and jammed it against the Edinburger's side. The pair of needle-sharp spikes pierced suit and clothes and bit into his flesh, and when the hilt slammed against his body the circuit was closed. The handle of the lightning prod was filled with powerful capacitors that released their stored electricity in a single

immense charge through the needles. The Edinburger writhed and died instantly.

They used his body to push a way into the
crowd.

Dom had just enough sensation left in his injured leg to be aware when the clamped-on nipoff
was twisted in his flesh by the men about them; he
kept his thoughts from what it was doing to his
leg.

Once the Edinburger soldiers were aware of the
open door they pulled it wide and fought their way
through it. The combatmen would be waiting for
them in the engine room. The sudden exodus relieved the pressure of the bodies for a moment and
Dom, with Pimenov struggling after him, pushed
and worked his way toward the MT controls.

It was like trying to move in a dream. The dark
bulk of the MT screen was no more than ten yards
away, yet they couldn't seem to reach it. Soldiers
sprang from the screen, pushing and crowding in,
more and more, preventing any motion in that direction. Two technicians stood at the controls,
their helmet phones plugged into the board before
them. Without gravity to push against, jammed
into the crowd that floated at all levels in a fierce
tangle of arms and legs, movement was almost
impossible. Pimenov touched his helmet to Dom's.

"I'm going ahead to cut a path. Stay close
behind me."

He broke contact before Dom could answer him,
then let his power ax pull him forward into the
press. Then he began to chop it back and forth in a
short arc, almost hacking his way through the
packed bodies. Men turned on him but he did not

stop, lashing out with his gropener as they tried to fight. Dom followed.

They were close to the MT controls before the combatman was buried under a crowd of stabbing, cursing Edinburgers. He had done his job and he died doing it. Dom jetted his gropener and let it drag him forward until he slammed into the thick steel frame of the MT screen above the operators' heads. He slid the weapon back into its sheath and used both hands to pull down along the frame, dragging himself headfirst through the press of suited bodies. There was a relatively clear space near the controls. He drifted down into it and let his drillger slide into the operator's back. The man writhed and died quickly. The other operator turned and took the weapon in his stomach. His face was just before Dom as his eyes widened and he screamed soundlessly with pain and fear. Nor could Dom escape the dead, horrified features as he struggled to drop the atomic bomb from his carrier. The murdered man stayed, pressed close against him all the time.

Now.

He cradled the bomb against his chest and, in a single swift motion, pulled out the arming pin, twisted the fuse to five seconds, and slammed down hard on the actuator. Then he reached up and switched the MT from *receive* to *send*.

The last soldiers erupted from the screen and there was a growing gap behind them. Into this space and through the screen he threw the bomb.

After that he kept the switch down and tried not to think about what was happening among the men

of the invasion army who were waiting before the
MT screen on that distant planet.

Then he had to hold this position until the
combatmen arrived. He sheltered behind the operator's corpse and used his drillger against the few
Edinburgers who were close enough to realize that
something had gone wrong. This was easy enough
to do because, although they were soldiers, they
were men from the invasion army and knew nothing about null-G combat. Very soon after this
there was a great stir and the closest ones were
thrust aside. An angry combatman blasted through,
sweeping his power ax toward Dom's neck. Dom
dodged the blow and switched his radio to combat
frequency.

"Hold that! I'm Corporal Priego, bomb squad.
Get in front of me and keep anyone else from
making the same mistake."

The man was one of those who had taken the
engine room. He recognized Dom now and nodded, turning his back to him and pressing against
him. More combatmen stormed up to form an iron
shield around the controls. The engineer pushed
through between them and Dom helped him reset
the frequency on the MT screen.

After this the battle became a slaughter and soon
ended.

"Sendout!" Dom radioed as soon as the setting
was made, then turned the screen to transmit. He
heard the words repeated over and over as the
combatmen repeated the withdrawal signal so that
everyone could hear it. Safety lay on the other side
of the screen, now that it was tuned to Tycho
Barracks on the Moon.

It was the Edinburgers, living, dead, and wounded who were sent through first. They were pushed back against the screen to make room for the combatmen who were streaming into the hold. The ones at the ends of the screen simply bounced against the hard surface and recoiled; the receiving screen at Tycho was far smaller than this great invasion screen. They were pushed along until they fell through and combatmen took up positions to mark the limits of the operating screen.

Dom was aware of someone in front of him and he had to blink away the red film that was trying to cover his eyes.

"Wing," he said, finally recognizing the man. "How many others of the bomb squad made it?"

"None I know of, Dom. Just me."

No, don't think about the dead. Only the living counted now.

"All right. Leave your bomb here and get on through. One is all we really need." He tripped the release and pulled the bomb from Wing's rack before giving him a push toward the screen.

Dom had the bomb clamped to the controls when Sergeant Toth slammed up beside him and touched helmets.

"Almost done."

"Done now," Dom said setting the fuse and pulling out the arming pin.

"Then get moving. I'll take it from here."

"No you don't. My job." He had to shake his head to make the haze go away but it still remained at the corners of his vision.

Toth didn't argue. "What's the setting?" he asked.

"Five and six. Five seconds after actuation the chemical bomb blows and knocks out the controls. One second later the atom bomb goes off."

"I'll stay to watch the fun."

Time was acting strangely for Dom, speeding up and slowing down. Men were hurrying by, into the screen, first in a rush, then fewer and fewer. Toth was talking on the combat frequency but Dom had switched the radio off because it hurt his head. The great chamber was empty now of all but the dead, with the automatic machine guns left firing at the entrances. One of them blew up as Toth touched helmets.

"They're all through. Let's go."

Dom had difficulty talking so he nodded instead and hammered his fist down onto the actuator.

Men were coming toward them but Toth had his arm around him, and full jets on his power ax were sliding them along the surface of the screen. And through.

When the brilliant lights of Tycho Barracks hit his eyes Dom closed them, and this time the red haze came up, over him, all the way.

"How's the new leg?" Sergeant Toth asked. He slumped lazily in the chair beside the hospital bed.

"I can't feel a thing. Nerve channels blocked until it grows tight to the stump." Dom put aside the book he had been reading and wondered what Toth was doing here.

"I come around to see the wounded," the sergeant said, answering the unasked question. "Two more besides you. Captain told me to."

"The captain is as big a sadist as you are. Aren't we sick enough already?"

"Good joke." His expression did not change. "I'll tell the captain. He'll like it. You going to buy out now?"

"Why not?" Dom wondered why the question made him angry. "I've had a combat mission, the medals, a good wound. More than enough points to get my discharge."

"Stay in. You're a good combatman when you stop thinking about it. There's not many of them. Make it a career."

"Like you, Sergeant? Make killing my life's work? Thank you, no. I intend to do something different, a little more constructive. Unlike you I don't relish this whole dirty business, the killing, the outright plain murder. You like it." This sudden thought sent him sitting upright in the bed. "Maybe that's it. Wars, fighting, everything. It has nothing to do anymore with territory rights or aggression or masculinity. I think that you people make wars because of the excitement of it, the thrill that nothing else can equal. You *like* war."

Toth rose, stretched easily, and turned to leave. He stopped at the door, frowning in thought.

"Maybe you're right, Corporal. I don't think about it much. Maybe I do like it." His face lifted in a cold tight smile. "But don't forget—you like it, too."

Dom went back to his book, resentful of the intrusion. His literature professor had sent him the book, along with a flattering note. He had heard about Dom on the broadcasts and the entire school was proud, etc. A book of poems, Milton, really good stuff.

> No war, or battle's sound
> Was heard the world around.

Yes, great stuff. But it hadn't been true in Milton's day and it still wasn't true. Did mankind really like war? They *must* like it or it wouldn't have lasted so long. This was an awful, criminal thought.

He, too? Nonsense. He fought well, but only because he had trained himself. It could not be true that he actually liked all of that.

He tried to read again but the page kept blurring before his eyes.

➤ *WIFE TO THE LORD*

HER NAME WAS OSIE and all agreed that she was by far the loveliest girl in the settlement of Wirral-Lo, a place that had been long known for the stunning beauty of its women. Wirral-Lo, perched on the high saddle of the inhospitable mountains of the planet called Orriols had little else to offer. Her beauty was a considerable asset and well guarded. When Osie ventured out of doors she wore a cloak of even heavier leadcloth than anyone else, as well as a wide-brimmed hat and thick dark glasses, all to protect her from the hard radiation of the burning blue-white sun. Inside, in the evenings, everyone appreciated the resulting fairness of her skin, the shine of her long black hair, the round bare perfection of her up-pointed full breasts. At these times her arms were covered—there were strict rules about that—and the overlapping layers of her full skirt chimed with little silver bells, while her

eyes hid always behind round dark glasses. But
what could be seen was very lovely and the workers, with the burnt patches on their faces and
necks, skin cancer scars and keloids, exacted a
great pleasure from looking at her unmarred beauty.
They were all very sad when it was decided that
she would be sent away to school.

This would be costly, but everyone looked upon
it as a good investment. Centuries earlier they had
emigrated to this patch of land to grow the pilloy
plants which ripened only in the Orriols soil under
the harsh actinic sun. The air was thin, but their
ancestors had lived for centuries in the great heights
of the South American mountains so this was no
hardship. Their chests were wide and deep and
they could breathe the air. But the hard radiation
was something else, and it had done them no
good. Their numbers had not increased the way
they should and there were never enough people to
work the land well. They needed expensive power
equipment, and the sale of the pilloy drug from the
plants never earned quite enough. So they were all
happy to make small sacrifices and to groom and
care for Osie because they knew that she would
fetch a very good bride price, indeed.

She was a young girl, fighting to control her
tears, when she waved goodby and stepped through
the matter transmitter and emerged in the city of
Bern, set within the mountains on Earth, to attend
her school. One year later to the day she reappeared from the screen, a poised young woman not
given to foolish tears of emotion.

At a great dinner, where all attended, this woman
they had known only as a girl was much admired.

Her manners were perfect, if slightly cool to them since they were only workers, her graceful beauty mature and breathtaking. She had a certificate from the school proclaiming that she had passed her courses with the highest grades, had impeccable social manners, had been trained in beauty culture, and was *virgo intactus* having never been out of sight of the school authorities during that entire year. She was ripe perfection. They looked with awe at the hair, the breasts, the perfect manners, and saw tractors, harrows, cultivators, and bag after bag of fertilizer.

"Here is the advertisement we will place," her father said after the last course and the tables had been cleared. There were shocked gasps, cries of approval.

"The picture—so perfect!"

"The measurements—exact to the centimeter!"

"The price—higher than any ever seen before!"

She looked down demurely into her wine glass and just a tiny smile touched her lips. A wave of affection passed over the tables and they would have kissed and hugged her with gratitude if there had not been some fear of damaging her, even slightly, or removing some of the *intactus*. She had never been kissed, even by her parents, since her fifth birthday. She was ready, ready.

Within three days the first answer came. There had been other answers of course, goodness knows how many, but the marriage journal had turned away all of those that could not meet the reserved price. A small squad of men in black came from the matter transmitter and looked about suspiciously as they were greeted in the rude hall that was the largest building, though they warmed considerably when Osie stepped gracefully before them. The lawyers among them scrutinized her papers, the doctors examined her under the watchful eyes of her people, and the business manager argued the price. It was all going very well indeed until another man stepped from the screen and stamped a booted foot.

"You, strangers, clear out. She will be my bride."

The men in black grew coldfaced and watched while Osie's father addressed the caller. He was quite polite since the man obviously had money. A lot of it. His clothes were of the richest fabrics, his jewelry, simple diamonds and emeralds, of a size and cut that were quite astonishing. His blond hair, silken soft and shoulder length, blended into his graceful mustaches, which he touched lightly with his knuckle.

"Might I inquire your name?" Osie's father asked, with a small bow that seemed right for the occasion.

"Well you might. I am Jochann, only Lord of Maabarot. I seek your daughter for my Lady."

That no one present had heard of Maabarot was not strange because since the advent of matter transmission mankind had spread through the galaxy like chaff before a wind and many were the worlds that were inhabited.

"We were here first," one of the lawyers said. "You will leave."

"I will stay," Jochann said, and flipped his ornate swagger stick with his fingertips. It was apparently well weighted and far heavier than it looked because it rapped the lawyer on the temple and the man dropped instantly unconscious to the floor.

"I will match their offer and go ten thousand credits more," Jochann said, and pulled a large bundle of currency from his wallet and dropped it on the table. "Not only that, but the obese creature these jackals represent is seventy years old with the skin of a warthog."

"Is this true?" Osie asked, speaking for the first time, and her clear voice rang in the same register as the bells upon her skirt.

"Not at all true!" one of the remaining lawyers said, keeping well back out of range. "You can see yourself, from this picture."

"True enough for me," Osie said, dropping the picture with the slightest curl to her delicate lips. She ground it underfoot as she turned to face Jochann.

"You may have me, my Lord, but I do not come cheap. For this basic price I will be yours, but never in spirit because I will always think that you put your money before your love. I ask you to be generous—"

"How generous?"

"At least fifty thousand credits more."

"This generosity is not cheap."

"Neither is my love. I see in you the kind of man I could love with passion and I feel that I would enjoy doing that. But I can do it only if I do not grieve for the poor state of my people. Pay them this small sum and you will find a new life of passion opening up for you."

She took one step forward, raised his unresisting

hand with hers, turned it palm up and bent forward to touch it with the tip of her pointed tongue. Jochann groaned aloud and fumbled in his wallet.

"I am convinced," he said, hurling bundle after bundle of currency onto the table, scarcely aware of what he was doing. "Prepare the marriage papers. Let the ceremony be done. I cannot wait long."

"I have been waiting for years," she said into his ear, in a voice as husky as his. "Saving up my passion for you."

He groaned again and sought action chasing the black-frocked men from the room, hurling the last one bodily into the matter transmitter.

Then Jochann regained his control and went stolidly through the marriage ceremony, signing all the forms and giving his bride a cool peck upon the cheek. But he would not stay for the planned banquet.

"Flesh can stand but so much," he said through tight-clenched teeth, and rooted in his seemingly exhaustless wallet for some more money. "I hope an additional payment will stay your grief at our nonattendance of this function, but stern duty calls. We must go."

They understood and were filled with compassion. Osie's bags appeared and, after Jochann had punched out his number, shielding the keys with his body, were pushed through the transmitter. He nodded goodby, gave his bride his arm, and they stepped through as well.

The room they stepped out into was small, windowless, dusty, and barren. Osie, with mannered perfection, said nothing. She watched with

casual interest as her new husband secured a great
lock on the transmitter controls, unbolted the door,
and led her into another room. The heavy door
was then closed behind them and secured with a
good half-dozen more locks. If this action puzzled
her she did not comment upon it, but looked around
at the large and tastefully furnished room, the
focus of attention of which was a great bed with
turned-back sheets.

"I knew you would be my bride," he grated,
half choked with passion, his arms about her,
leaning her toward the bed. In an instant he realized her body was hard as a board, unyielding, her
expression blank. He reluctantly released her and
she straightened her clothing before she spoke.

"You will have my bags brought to my robing
room and have me shown where it is. I will prepare myself carefully because this should not be
done with unseemly haste. Prepare yourself as
well because it will be two or three days at least
before you leave this room."

While she spoke she slowly raised the black
glasses that always concealed her eyes and they
were wide and dark and deep with such promise of
passion that he almost drowned in their depths.
Then her lips burnt with fire on his, then they were
gone, and he nodded, incapable of speech, and
pointed wordlessly to a door set into the far wall.

The first week went very well for Osie. The
school in the Alps of Earth had trained her well, as
well as they could without practical lessons, and
she found she had a natural aptitude for this sort of
thing. Besides that, it was a relief to change her

status at last. The only pleasure she had previously enjoyed was anticipation, which is rather unsatisfactory over a period of years. So now she used all the exercises she had been taught, that first day and night, and then the various restimulating exotica prescribed for waning powers, and it was more than seven days in all before she awoke and found her husband gone from the marital couch. She yawned and stretched, sated and at peace with the world, and pressed the button beside the bed.

Previously the curtains had been drawn and invisible hands had silently delivered the desired food and drink. This time she drew back the draperies and watched, relaxed against the pillows, as an attractive girl in serving costume came hesitantly into the room.

"Some wine," she ordered. "Light, cool, and refreshing, and something to eat. What do you suggest?"

The maid mutely hung her head.

"Come, come, it is all right to speak. I am your mistress and wife of the Lord. So, what food?"

The girl shook her head dumbly and Osie began to feel anger.

"Speak up, you are not mute."

To which the girl responded by nodding her head vigorously and pointing to her throat.

"You poor thing," Osie said, instantly compassionate. "And so young and pretty, too. Then bring me something nice, I do believe that I have quite an appetite."

The food arrived and she ate well, afterward enjoying a long bath and the languid pleasures of doing her nails and hair. She had a lifetime to see this world, her new home, and was in no hurry. Her husband would undoubtedly enjoy showing it to her and she wanted his pleasure as well. This marriage had a fortuitous beginning.

Toward evening the tall bronze doors were thrown wide and Jochann entered striding firmly. He was an immensely strong man so he did not appear fatigued, though it must be admitted that there were deep-cut dark circles under his eyes. Osie raised her arms and they kissed, but he stepped back swiftly as he felt the warm tides of passion arising once again.

"Enough, at least for the moment," he said. "My wife, I must show you something of your world, and the people of Maabarot will want to see their Lady. If you will dress in something unusually fine we will step out onto a balcony and wave to the throng that has been gathering for three days, their enthusiasm undiminished by time." He touched a button on the wall and the roar of countless throats could be heard.

"They sound pleased."

"It is a great event in their lives. After the balcony we shall go to a dinner where you will meet the higher-placed people of this world. Before you do that, there is something I must tell you."

Jochann paced back and forth, his fingers working unknowingly at the gold threads of his tunic, a frown—was it of apprehension?—wrinkling his brow.

"You have some confession perhaps? Something you did not want to tell me until we were

safely married?'' There was a certain coldness to
her words.

"My love!" He dropped to his knees before
her, taking her hands in his. "Nothing like that, I
assure you. I am the Lord of Maabarot as I told
you. All the resources of this rich planet are mine
and I will share every part of them with you. I
have concealed nothing. Other than my people's
attitude toward me."

"They do not like you?"

"Quite the opposite. They adore me." He rose,
dusted his knees and when his chin was raised his
face became set in an expression of calm nobility.
"In fact they rather venerate me. You must understand that they are simple people and they look
upon me with a certain awe."

"How very nice. Perhaps as did the ancient
Egyptians, or Japanese, they consider you an offspring of the sun god?"

"Like that, only a bit better."

"What could be better?"

"They believe that I *am* God."

"How very nice," she told him, showing only
interest and no signs of laughter, disbelief, or
scoffing, since the Bern school had been a good
one.

"Yes it is. A burden of course since my slightest whim is law and I must not disabuse that
power."

"Do *you* believe that you are God?"

"Well you might ask!" He smiled. "Logically,
as a man of science, of course not." He frowned.
"Though at times I have strange feelings. The

pressure of their utter belief is so strong. But we will talk of that some other time.''

"Would you mind telling me how this situation came about?''

"I'm a little vague on the earlier details myself. Some remote ancestor of mine came into possession of the only matter transmitter on this world and in some way concealed its existence from the people. To the uneducated the things this device can accomplish do seem miraculous. Tons of grain vanish into a tiny room far smaller than their total bulk. Strange and wondrous devices appear in their place. Maabarot dozes away the centuries in a paternistically feudal twilight and the only man with any knowledge of science is the Lord God, myself. And of course the Lord's wife, miraculously appeared from heaven to be his consort. A Lord's wife is always from another planet. A Lord has but one son, who becomes God in his father's place when the elder Lord returns to heaven. You will have but one son. You will have no daughters.''

"I shall miss them. I always did like big families.''

"I am sorry. But you will obey me without rancor?''

"Of course. Did I not swear to obey you? Instead of a large family I shall lavish my not inconsiderable love on my single son, which is only right considering that some day he will be God. I am not displeased.''

"Wonderful! My wife is a jewel in ten million. Shall we to the balcony?''

"I will call the maid to dress me. What is her name?''

"Bacjli."

"How did she lose her powers of speech?"

"I told her she could no longer speak, therefore she cannot. The people sincerely believe in God on this planet. The house servants are illiterate and cannot speak, therefore can reveal none of the secrets and details of existence here."

"Is this necessary?"

"It is the law and the way it always has been. I am as bound to it as they are. They believe it a small sacrifice, and thousands vie for positions in my palace."

"There are many things that I must become used to."

"Being wife to God is second in difficulty only to being God."

"How nicely you phrase it."

The reception that greeted the new Lady when she stepped out onto the balcony was chaotic and passed quickly into hysteria when she condescended to speak to them. But the Lord raised his hand and ordered that peace descend on his people and it did. Partly because of the power of suggestion but mostly because he released tranquilizing gas into the crowd by operating the remote control unit fastened to his belt. The divine couple descended to the banquet flushed with excitement and entered to the wail of trumpets to see a sea of bent backs. Once God and his mate had been seated the nobility straightened up and stepped forward, one at a time as the seneschal called their names, to genuflect and kiss the ring that Osie wore. She sipped iced wine all the while and smiled, counterpoint to

Jochann's godly grimness, and they all loved her with their entire hearts. God, tired of the introductions, halted them with a raised finger and the meal began.

It was a delicious repast that never got past the seventeenth course, which consisted of tiny birds roasted in honey. The seneschal reappeared and silence fell as he rapped his staff of office loudly on the marble floor.

"Oh God, Father of us all, who rules with lightning and love, we beg to inform You that Your high court is at this time rendering justice."

"I shall come," he said, rising and offering his arm to Osie. "Hell, right in the middle of the meal. But it is one of those things that just has to be done. God can't skimp his work, you know. The walk may help our appetites so all is not lost."

The guests bowed and backed away, then followed their Lord and His Lady, in a murmuring crowd, to the Palace of Justice where the high court sat. Jochann led his bride to a small balcony, tastefully decorated with plaster clouds to resemble a seat in heaven. They sat on plush thrones while the judges filed in, black garbed and cloaked in righteousness like all judges everywhere. The clerk spoke in a high tenor, half singing the words.

"The judges return. The defendant will rise."

For the first time Osie noticed a bald man in torn gray clothing who sat in a spike-guarded box. He was so burdened with chains that the soldiers had to help him to his feet. Then they stepped back to their positions leaving him swaying alone.

"Prisoner," the clerk sang, "you have been

accused of the most awful crime known to man. You have sinned badly, damning yourself from your own mouth. You are guilty of heresy. You have denied the existence of God and the judges will now pass sentence.''

"I'll say it again!" the defendant shouted in a cracked, hoarse voice. "I'll say it right to his face, I will. He is no more God than I am. A man, just a man!''

The crowd howled and pressed forward seeking his blood, and the many guards fought to restrain him.

"My fault," God told his wife. "The market for farm products keeps falling and I have tried to modernize the economy. I've had a pilot plant built for the manufacture of electronic components. But science is a curse in a feudal society. This man was supervisor there and his technical know-how has led him into theological sin.''

"Will you show mercy?" she asked, frightened by the blood lust of the crowd.

"I cannot, for I am a stern God and must be feared.''

The judges rose and chanted together.

"We, the judges, find the defendant guilty as charged, and do surrender him to the hands of the living God. To die at once, let justice prevail!''

"Justice!" the prisoner screeched as Jochann slowly rose, his words clear in the breathless hush. "Superstition, that's all it is. Suggestion, make me think I'm going to die. But I won't do it, no sir. I'm not going to drop dead just because he says die—''

"Die," Jochann intoned and leveled his finger.

The man screamed, writhed horribly in his chains, and died.

"How terrible," Osie said. "The power of suggestion . . . ?"

"Works with most of them. But I take precautions with the hard cases. Fifty thousand volts wired right through those chains. Remote control. Let's go back before the food gets cold."

For some reason Osie had no more appetite and left the banquet after sipping some more wine. In her dressing room she prepared herself for the rest of the evening's festivities while she tried to forget the recent events. But she could not. Then she tried to rationalize the execution and did much better. Obedience to the law and the constituted authorities. Without obedience we would have only chaos. She convinced herself well enough to greet her husband, God, with renewed passion when he returned. God's in his bedroom, all's right with the world.

"I believe I am what is called a benevolent despot," Jochann said next day as they rode side by side through the streets of the town below the castle. Stout bearers carried their palanquin on husky shoulders and spear-carrying soldiers kept the cheering crowd at bay. Jochann nodded to each side as he talked, smiling automatically, and throwing out handfuls of coins of small denomination.

"How very nice for you," Osie said, bestowing smiles as well, "and for me too, of course. But are the people happy?"

"As pigs in a parsley patch. Because I really am benevolent. They have all of the benefits of science without the foul byproducts or responsibilities. No smog, no pollution, no industry. No endless years at school to compete for a place in a technocratic society. No schools for that matter, so happy children are everywhere. Maabarot is a paradise and they are appropriately grateful.''

"You have a crime problem?''

"None. People obey the law when a living God is looking over their shoulders.''

"They are not hungry?''

"Food and clothing and shelter for all by God's law.''

"They are not sick?''

"The temples, fitted with the most modern chirurgical and medical machines cure them all. Miraculously. They are appropriately grateful.''

"They complain about nothing.''

"Nothing. The skies ring with hosannahs. They live in paradise and are in no hurry to get to heaven.''

"The man who died . . . ?''

"A malcontent. They are very few. On the bell-shaped curve of happiness there are always a handful on the downslope who grumble at paradise. But even in dying they serve a function by setting an example for the happy hordes. Fat, sunburned, well fed, stupid. They want for nothing. Hear how they acclaim me!''

And shout they did. And weep with joy and hold up their children to be blessed and kiss the ground over which He had passed and swoon with passion. It was all very satisfactory. In the Street of Goldsmiths priceless trinkets were forced upon them. In the Bazaar of Jewelers cut stones fell like precious rain. Their visit was a triumph, and they returned breathless with pleasure, drank cool wine, and before they knew it were celebrating the triumph with greater triumphs in bed.

Time fled by. When the pastoral pleasures palled they would slip away to another planet for the theater or a concert or other civilized entertainment. Not often, for here there was yachting, riding, climbing, banqueting, hunting, fishing, endless opportunities for sport and joy. A week, a month, and then a year slipped by unnoticed and in the privacy of their bedchamber, after the great celebratory banquet, Jochann took her hand in his and, after kissing it, said, "It is time to think about our heir."

"I have been thinking about him and wondering when the blessed event might occur."

"Nine months from now if you agree with me."

"I do," she said and threw her jar of pills through the open window. "Shall we begin?"

"Not quite yet. We must return to Earth to the *Vereinigte Vielseitgkeit Fruchtbarkeit Krankenhaus* in Zurich. The most famous fertility clinic in all the worlds."

"You have doubts about my fertility?" she asked in a voice with a cold steel edge to it.

"Never, my love, never! I have no doubt that from your fruitful womb could spring girls, twins, quintuplets; you are capable of anything."

"I understand." She kissed him. "One boy. Shall we go?"

"I'll dial the number now."

It was more like a birth than a conception and Jochann paced the waiting room floor for long hours before he was summoned. The doctor was bald and emotionless and reading from the report.

"Male offspring, one, no broken genes, selected from finest traits available, now passed the third cell division and growing fast. Congratulations, it is going to be a boy."

Jochann pumped the doctor's hand, tears of gratitude in his eyes.

"I can never thank you too much, Doctor. When may I see my wife?"

"Now."

"When may I see my son?"

"In nine months."

"You have made me a very happy man."

"There is one danger, however."

"Danger!" God almost swooned at the word and held tight to his chair for support. "What do you mean?" he cried.

"There is nothing that cannot be avoided if you take the proper precautions. Your wife is from a planet with a very rarefied atmosphere and her strain has been adjusted to this through many generations. She has no difficulty accommodating to a denser atmosphere, but there is some danger to the offspring during pregnancy. You must take precautions. Can she return to her home world until the child is born?"

"Impossible! Her world is now my world."

"Are you a rich man?"

"Incredibly so. Does it make a difference?"

"It does. You must find a mountain on your planet where the air pressure is her norm and build her a small villa there where she can pass the coming months."

"I will build her a castle, gardens, a world of beauty, with a thousand servants and a private hospital."

"A small villa will do fine, but I imagine she will not object to your arrangements. Here is your bill and you may see your wife as soon as you pay it."

He wrote the outsize check in a golden haze of happiness. Then he found Osie, and they embraced in a climax of shared joy. Hand in hand they returned, summoned the servants and set off at once for the mountains.

It was a picnic of pleasure. When the heavily laden procession came to a town the inhabitants all joined it to share the burdens a part of the way. They rolled over the foothills and up the flank of the Great Divide. When Jochann's golden barometer pinged he struck his staff into the ground and shouted, "This is the place."

In the mountain meadow there, looking out over a green valley with the ice-topped mountains as a backdrop, the palace was constructed. They camped in a silken pavilion while the people labored with pleasure. Swiftly the building rose and was surrounded by gardens and fountains and music, and a great celebration was held when it was done.

"My darling, I must return to the palace to work," he told her in the privacy of their bed that night.

"I shall miss you, truly. Will you return soon?"

"As quickly as I can. But when there is only one true God He cannot rest."

"I know. I shall be waiting."

The nine months passed quickly and Jochann

had horse stations established along the route so he
could travel post haste between the two palaces.
He had planned to be there for the delivery, but he
was detained on business and his son surprised
him by an early arrival. The first inkling he had of
the unexpected, though still blessed, event was
when a breathless and dusty messenger staggered
into the throne room and sprawled before him
holding up, with his last bit of strength, the forked
stick with the message. Jochann read it and the
universe reeled.

Come it said *at once. Your wife has given birth
and both are fine but something of interest has
happened*.

What chilled his blood was the apparent haste
with which the note had been written and dispatched, and the fact something else had been
written in place of "of interest" and then scratched
out. When he held it to the light he saw that the
word was *strange*.

He killed three horses during that historic ride,
and almost himself when an expiring mount col-
lapsed at the edge of a cliff. But made it he did
and burst open the door of the completely equipped
and staffed hospital and seized the doctor by his
coat and lifted him wriggling into the air.

"What has happened?" he shouted, hoarse-voiced
and filthy, red-eyed with fatigue.

"Nothing, they are both fine," said the doctor,
and would say no more until released.

"Your wife is fine, your son is fine. She wants
to talk to you now and the nurse will help you
clean up before you enter her room."

Chagrined, he submitted to the ministrations of

the off-planet nurse hired for this occasion, then tiptoed in to Osie's room. They kissed and she smiled and patted the bed beside her.

"It has all been wonderful. Your son is blue-eyed and blond-haired, like his father, with a great voice and force of will. He is without infirmities and perfect in every way."

"I must see him!"

"The nurse is bringing him now. But first I must ask you something."

"Anything."

"During my studies I read about theology and understood that man had made God in his own image."

"It is usually quoted the other way around, but that is true."

"Therefore if people believe strongly enough and hard enough that there is a God there will be a God."

"It could be argued that way. Could we have this theological discussion later since I admit to being distracted somewhat?"

"I am finished. And here is your son."

The baby was perfect as they had said. Already smiling and clenching small fists.

They had not told him that there was something else.

Floating, just four centimeters above his head, moving when he moved, was a shining silver loop of light.

➤ *WAITING PLACE*

As SOON AS Jomfri stepped out of the screen of the
matter transmitter, he realized that there had been
a terrible mistake. For one thing his head hurt with
a pain that almost blinded him, a classic symptom
of MT malfunction. For another this was not his
destination, not this gray and dusty chamber. He
had been on his way home. Staggering, his arm
before his eyes, he felt his way to the hard bench
that was secured to one wall. He sat, slumped,
with his head on his hands, and waited for the pain
to ooze away.

The worst was over, that was certain, and he
should be thankful that he had survived. Jomfri
knew all about MT failures from the 3V plays
since, though rare in reality, these dramatic circumstances were natural material for the robot
scripters. The failure of a single microscopic circuit would be enough to send the hapless traveler

to a receiver that was not the one that he had punched for, while at the same time giving his nervous system a random twist that accounted for the headache. This was what the technicians called a minimal malfunction, and once the headache had faded the victim could punch for the local emergency station, report the malfunction, then go on. The worst that could happen was too horrifying to consider: people who arrived turned inside out or stretched in one dimension into miles of tubular flesh. Or even worse. He was all right, Jomfri told himself, clutching his head with both hands, he had come through all right.

When he opened one eye a crack the light hurt, but was bearable. He could stand, shakily, and see, barely, so it was time to get help. They would have drugs in the emergency station that would fix his head. And he had to report the malfunctioning transmitter before anyone else was caught in the thing. His fingers groped over the featureless wall for clumsy seconds trying to find the punch panel.

"It is impossible!" Jomfri cried, his eyes wide open despite the pain. "There is always a panel."

There was none. This screen was for receiving only. It was theoretically possible that a MT screen could be one way, without a sending tuner, but he had never seen one before. "Outside," he said, turning from the blank screen in this blank room.

Leaning against the featureless wall for support Jomfri went out the door and down a barren hallway. The hall made a single right-angled turn and opened into a dust-filled street. A scrap of dirty plastic blew by and there was the smell of warm decay.

"The sooner I'm away from this place the better. I'll find another transmitter." Then he moaned as the sunlight struck daggers of pain through his eyes and into his brain. He made his way into the street, stumbling, peering through the smallest crack between the fingers that he clamped tight over his eyes. Tears ran down his cheeks, and through his damp agony he searched the blank, gray walls for the familiar red double-headed MT arrow. It was nowhere to be seen. A man sat in a doorway, his face hidden in the shadows.

"Help me," Jomfri said. "I'm hurt. I must find the MT station—where is it?" The man shuffled his feet but said nothing. "Can't you understand?" Jomfri was petulant. "I'm in pain. Your duty as a citizen. . . ."

Still in silence, the man caught his toe behind Jomfri's ankle, then slammed him in the knee with his other foot. Jomfri went down, and the stranger stood at the same time. "Dirty fangner," he said and kicked Jomfri hard in the groin, then stalked away.

It was a long time before Jomfri could do more than lie, curled up and moaning, afraid to move, as though he were a cracked egg that would burst and spill its contents if disturbed. When he did sit up finally, wiping feebly at the sour bile on his lips, he was aware that people had passed him, yet none had stopped. He did not like this city, this planet, wherever he was. He wanted to leave. Standing was painful, and walking even more so, yet he did it. Find the MT station, get out, find a doctor. Leave.

In other circumstances Jomfri might have re-

marked on the barrenness of this place, with its
lack of vehicular traffic, its scattering of pedestri-
ans and its complete lack of signs and street names,
as though illiteracy had been established by edict.
But now the only concern he had for his surroundings was to leave them. Passing an arcaded opening he stopped and cautiously, for he had learned
discretion with that single kick, he looked inside.
It was a courtyard with rough tables scattered about,
planks nailed to their legs in lieu of benches. Some
of them were occupied. A small barrel rested on
the central table, at which sat six men and a
woman, filling cups from it. All present were as
drab as the walls about them, dressed for the most
part in uniform gray, although some of them had
parts of their costume made up of drab pastels.

Jomfri drew back quickly as the woman came
toward him, then realized that she was lank-haired
and old, keeping her eyes to the ground as she
shuffled forward, carrying the plastic cup in both
hands. She slid onto one of the benches close by
and buried her face in her drink.

"Can you help me?" Jomfri asked, sitting at the
far corner of the table where she could neither kick
nor hit him and where he could flee if he had to.

She looked up, startled, and pulled the cup to
her. When he made no further movements toward
her she blinked her red-rimmed eyes, while a mottled tip of tongue licked out at her cracked lips and
withdrew.

"Will you help?" he asked again, feeling safe
enough for the moment.

"New one here," she said, her words hissing

and blurring over her toothless gums. "Don't like it, do you?"

"No, I certainly do not like it, and I'm going to leave. If you would direct me to the nearest MT station—"

The crone cackled hoarsely then sipped loudly from her cup. "One way only, fangner; you knew that before they sent you. The road to Fangnis has but one direction."

At the sound of this time-weary cliché he gasped and suddenly felt very cold. Memories of the priest with the raised, admonitory finger: the father to his errant daughter. Was there a Fangnis? "It cannot be," he said in a futile effort to convince himself differently, while his eyes darted like trapped animals to the buildings, the street, the people, and back again.

"It is," the woman said, and he had the feeling she would drop her head to the table and weep, but she only drank again.

"There has been a dreadful mistake. I should not be here."

"Everyone says that," she said with contempt, dismissing him with a palsied wave of her hand. "You'll stop soon. Criminals all, rejected from our own worlds, sentenced for life and eternity, forgotten. They used to kill us. It would have been kinder."

"I have heard of Fangnis," Jomfri said hurriedly. "A world no one knows where, eternal noon." He shot a frightened glance at the changeless light in the street outside, then away. "The unwanted, the condemned, the guilty, the incorrigible, the criminals are sent there. All right, *here* then," he added when he saw her twisted and humorless smile, "I'll not argue with you. Perhaps you are right. In any case there has been a grave mistake made, and it must be rectified. I am no criminal. I was on my way home from work. My wife will be waiting. I dialed my number and appeared . . . here."

She no longer looked at him, but stared numbly into her drink instead. He was suddenly aware of how dry his mouth was. "What are you drinking? Could I have some?"

The old woman roused at this, pulling the drink to her and cradling it against her ancient breasts. "Mine. I worked for it. You can drink water like all the other fangners. I cut the wood and watched the fire at the swamp-edge while it dripped. My share."

The cup was almost empty now, and he could smell the raw spirit on her breath when she talked. "Out there. Down the street. Go away. Food and water at the Warden. Go away." She had lost interest in him, and he rose painfully and left before there was any more trouble.

"The Warden, of course," he told himself with a sudden warm spurt of hope. "I'll explain and he'll take care of me."

Jomfri walked faster. The street ended in a dusty hillside, a smoothly rising, round-topped hill surrounded by the monotony of the low drab buildings. A structure clamped itself to the hilltop, a hemispherical and featureless dome of durcrete. Hard as diamond and as eternal. A thin man in rusty black and gray was trudging up the hill before him, and Jomfri followed furtively, ready to turn and run at any sign of hostility.

Water gushed continually from a durcrete spout and splashed into a drain below. The thin man secured a plastic bag over the spout, and when it filled he reached into a deep opening in the wall beside the spout and took out a blocky package of some kind. Jomfri waited until he had removed the filled bag and vanished around the curve of the dome before he went forward. The sibilance of the splashing water was the only sound in the hazy silence, and his throat was suddenly dry. He buried his head under the stream, let it run into his mouth and over his face and across his hands. When he pulled away, gasping for air, he felt much better. Wiping the water from his eyes, he pushed his head into the opening. It was almost featureless. A shiny, worn metal plate was inset to his right, and a hole, no bigger around than his arm, vanished upward into darkness from the farther end of the pit. The word PRESS, almost completely rubbed away, was printed above the plate. The only letters he had seen since he arrived here. Hesitatingly, he put his thumb to the cool metal. There was a distant susurration and a rising, scraping sound. Jomfri pulled his hand out quickly as a plastic-wrapped package shot down out of the opening and plopped softly into the rear of the niche. He took it out and saw that it was a bag of mealpaste.

"Go ahead, eat, I won't bother you."

Jomfri spun about, almost dropping the bag, to face the thin man who had silently returned to stand close behind him. "You're new here, I could tell,'' the man said, and a wholly artificial smile passed over his lined and pock-marked face. "Say hello to Old Rurry, I can be your friend.''

"Take this,'' Jomfri said, extended the mealpaste, trying to push away all connection with Fangnis. "There has been a mistake; this is someone else's ration; the machine gave it to me in error. I do not belong here.''

"Of course not, young fangner,'' Old Rurry purred. "Many is the life ended by politicians, innocent men sent here. The machine doesn't care or know who is here or who you are or who I am. It has a five-hour memory and won't feed you again until that time has passed. It will feed anyone, every five hours, forever. That is the sort of horrible efficiency that makes one squirm, isn't it?''

Jomfri's fingers clutched spasmodically, digging deep into the flexible wrapping. "No, I am sincere. A mistake in the MT sent me here. If you really wish to help me you will show me how to contact the authorities.''

Old Rurry shrugged and looked bored. "Impossible. They're sealed inside this tomb and come and go with their own MT. They never contact us. We feed at this side of the Warden—and leave at the other.''

"Leave? Then it is possible. Take me there.''

Sniffing wetly, Old Rurry wiped his nose on the back of his finger, then examined it carefully and wiped it on the side of his jacket before he spoke. "If you must be ghoulish, that can be easily enough arranged. Right there.'' He pointed the wiped finger at the foot of the hill where four men had appeared, carrying a woman face down, one to each limb. They plodded forward until they noticed the two men waiting above them, then the two men bearing the legs dropped them into the dirt, turned and left.

"A civic duty," Old Rurry said distastefully, "and the only one we perform. If we just leave them or dump them into the swamp they rot, and that is highly unpleasant." They walked down, and Old Rurry pointed silently to the left leg while he picked up the right. Jomfri hesitated, and all three fangners turned to stare coldly at him. He bent quickly—memory of that educatory boot—clutched the bare flesh of the ankle, almost dropping it again at the feel of its cold and firm, unfleshlike texture. They continued up the hill, and Jomfri turned away from the sight of the dirt-stained, blue-veined leg. Perhaps this was the woman he had talked to. He shuddered at the thought. No, the clothing was different, and this one was long dead.

A well-traveled dirt track ran about the circumference of the Warden, and they shuffled along it until they reached a spot that appeared to be diametrically opposite the feeding station. A long narrow strip of metal was inset in the wall at knee-height, perhaps a foot wide and eight feet long. The leading man on the inside bent and pulled at a groove in the metal. It swung out slowly to reveal that it was the outer side of a V-shaped bin. The bin was constructed of three-inch-thick armor alloy, yet was still dented and scratched along the edge. How desperate could one become after a lifetime in this place? The

body was unceremoniously dumped into the bin
and the outer door kicked shut.

"Unrivaled efficiency," Old Rurry said, watching warily as the two other men departed without a
word. "No communication, no contact. The end.
Bodies and old clothes. Their bodies are taken
away and new sack-cloth issued for old rags. Remember that when your fine clothes grow worn."

"This cannot be all!" Jomfri shouted, tugging
at the door which was now locked. "I must contact those inside and explain the error. I don't
belong in this place."

There was a slight vibration, he could feel it in
his fingertips; and the door yielded to his tugging.
It opened, and the bin was empty. In a frenzy of
haste Jomfri climbed in and stretched out full length.
"Close it, please, I beg," he said to Old Rurry
who bent over him. "This is all to no purpose,"
replied Old Rurry. Still, when Jomfri pleaded, he
pushed the door shut. The light narrowed to a
crack and vanished. The darkness was absolute.

"I am not dead," Jomfri shouted in sudden
panic. "Nor am I old clothes. Can you hear me? I
wish to report a mistake. I was on my way home,
you see, and—"

Soft bars, it felt like a dozen of them clamped
tight against his body. He screamed feebly, then
louder when something brushed against his head
and face. There was a tiny humming in the darkness.

"An incorrectly dialed number, a malfunction
in the MT. I am here in error. You must believe
me."

As silently as they had come the arms were
withdrawn. He felt about him, but there was solid

metal on all sides as though he were sealed in a coffin. Then a crack and a slit of light appeared, and he closed his eyes against the sudden glare. When he opened them again he looked up at Old Rurry, who was sucking the last of the foodpaste from a container.

"Yours," he said. "I didn't think you wanted it. Climb out of there, it won't move again until you do."

"What happened? Something held me."

"Machines. See if you are dead or sick or old clothes. If you're sick they give you a shot before they toss you back. You can't fool them. Only the dead go on through."

"They wouldn't even listen to me," he said, climbing wearily out.

"That's the whole idea. Modern penology. Society no longer kills or punishes the individual for trespassing its laws. The criminal is redeemed. Some cannot be. They are the ones who would have been hanged, burned, flayed, broken, electrocuted, beheaded, racked, speared, or otherwise executed in more barbarous times. Now they are simply dismissed from civilized society to enjoy the company of their peers. Could anything be more just? The condemned are sent here on a one-way journey. Away from the society they have offended, no longer a burden on it as they would be in a prison. A minimal contribution from all the worlds using this service supplies food and clothing and operating costs. Dismissed and forgotten— for there is no escape. We are on a clouded and primitive world, forever facing the unseen sun, surrounded by nothing but swamps. That is the all of it. Some survive, some die quickly. There is room for a hundred times our number without crowding. We eat, we sleep, we kill each other. Our only joint effort is the operation of stills at the swamp's edge. The local fruit is inedible, but it ferments. And alcohol is alcohol. Since you are a newcomer I will give you one drink of hospitality and welcome you into our drinking band. We've had too many deaths of late, and more wood is needed."

"No. I won't join your convict alcoholics. I'm different, I was sent here by mistake. Not like you."

Old Rurry smiled and, with a swiftness that denied his years, produced a shining blade that he pricked into Jomfri's throat.

"Learn this rule quickly. Never ask a man why he is here nor mention it to him. It is a messy form of suicide. I will tell you, because I am not ashamed. I was a chemist. I knew all the formulas. I made tasteless poison and killed my wife and eighty-three of her family. That makes eighty-four. Few here can match that number." He slid the knife back into his sleeve, and Jomfri backed away, rubbing the red mark on his neck.

"You're armed," he said, shocked.

"This is a world, not a prison. We do our best. Through the years bits of metal have accumulated, weapons have been manufactured. This knife must be generations old. The myth has it that it was made from an iron meteorite. All things are possible. I killed its former owner by thrusting a sharpened length of wire through his eardrum and into his brain."

"I do feel like that drink now. Thank you for offering. Very kind." Jomfri worked hard to give no offense. The old man started down the hill with Jomfri trailing after. The building they went to was like all the others.

"Very good," Jomfri said, choking over a beaker of the acid and acrid drink.

"Filthy stuff," Old Rurry told him. "I could improve it. Add natural flavoring. But the others won't let me. They know my record."

Jomfri took a deeper drink. He knew the record, too. When he finished the beaker his head was fuzzy and his stomach sickened. He felt no better. He knew that if he had to stay on Fangnis he would be one of the men who died swiftly. This life was worse than no life.

"Sick! You said they would see me if I were sick," he shouted, jumping to his feet. Old Rurry ignored him, and he was drunk enough to clutch the man by his clothing. None of the others paid particular attention until the wicked length of blade appeared again. Jomfri let go and staggered backward, his eyes on the foot of steel. "I want you to cut me with your knife," he said.

Old Rurry stopped and thought; he had never received an invitation from a prospective victim before. "Cut you where?" He scanned the other for a suitable spot.

"Where?" Where indeed. What part of one's body do you invite violence upon? What member that you have borne a lifetime do you discard? "A finger . . ." he suggested hesitantly.

"Two fingers—or none," Old Rurry told him, a natural merchant of destruction.

"Here then." Jomfri dropped into the chair and spread his hands before him. "Two, the littlest." He clenched his fists with the little fingers on the table edge. They were too far apart. He crossed his wrists so that the two little fingers hooked over the wooden edge, side by side. "Both at once. Can you do that?"

"Of course. Right at the second joint."

Old Rurry hummed happily to himself, noticing that the entire room was watching him now. He pretended to examine the edge of his blade while the newcomer looked up at him with watery rabbit's eyes. Fast, without warning, the knife came down and bit deep into the wood. The fingers flew, blood spurted, the newcomer shrieked. Everyone laughed uproariously as he ran out the door still screaming.

"Good Old Rurry," someone shouted, and he permitted himself a smile while he picked up one of the fingers from the floor.

"I'm hurt—now you must help me!" Jomfri shouted as he staggered up the hill in the endless noon. "I did not think it would feel like this. I'll bleed to death. I need your aid. It hurts so."

When he tugged at the metal the pain bit deep. The bin gaped open, and he dropped into it. "I'm injured," he wailed as the light narrowed and vanished. The bars clamped down in the darkness, and he could feel the warm blood running down his wrists. "That's blood. You must stop it, or I will die."

The mechanism believed. There was a sharp nip of pain in his neck, then instant numbness. The pain was gone from his body—as was all sensation. He could move his head, hear and talk, but was completely paralyzed from the neck down. There were no escapes from Fangnis.

Something rumbled, and from the sensation on the back of his head he knew he was being slid sideways by the mechanism. It was too dark to see—if he could still see at all—but from the movement of the air and the sounds, he felt that he was being moved through door after door, like a multi-chambered airlock. Thick metal doors, that would be certain. The last one slid open, and he was ejected into a well-lit room.

"Torture again," the man in white said, bending over to look. "They're going back to their old games." Behind him were three guards with thick clubs.

"Initiation, maybe, Doctor. This one must be a newcomer, I've never seen him before."

"And new clothes, too," the doctor said, working with swabs and instruments.

"I'm here by mistake. I'm not a prisoner!"

"If we get one, Doctor, we can look forward to a lot more amputation. They always do things in cycles."

"A mistake on the matter transmitter—"

"You're right about that. I have some graphs that prove it in the book I am preparing."

"Listen, you must listen. I was going home. I dialed my home, I went into the MT—and arrived here. There has been a ghastly mistake. I had the fingers removed so that I could reach you. Look at the records, they'll prove I'm right."

"We have records," the doctor admitted, recognizing Jomfri's humanity for the first time. "But

there has never been a mistake yet, though many
have claimed their innocence.''

"Doctor, please find out. I am begging you. In
the name of decency simply consult the records.
The computer will tell you instantly."

The doctor hesitated a moment, then shrugged.
"In the name of decency, then. I will do it while
the dressings set. Your name and citizen's number."

He punched Jomfri's data into the computer,
then looked expressionless at the screen.

"You see," Jomfri shouted happily. "It was a
mistake. I'll file no complaints. Free me now, it is
all I ask."

"You are guilty," the doctor said quietly. "You
were sent here."

"Impossible!" Jomfri was justifiably angry.
"Some trick. I demand you tell me what I have
been charged with."

The doctors looked at his instruments. "Blood
pressure, brain waves, normal for this situation.
These instruments are as good as any lie detector.
You are telling the truth. Traumatic amnesia, very
possible in this situation. A good footnote for my
book."

"Tell me what I have been accused of!" Jomfri
was shouting and trying to move.

"It would be better if you did not know. I'll
return you now."

"You must tell me first. I cannot believe you
otherwise. I was on my way home to my wife—"

"You killed your wife," the doctor said, and
actuated the return mechanism. The closing of the
thick door cut off the hideous, wailing scream.

A single sharp memory of a blue face, staring eyes, blood blood blood. . . .

The metal coffin lid opened, and Jomfri sat up, dizzy. They had drugged him; he was hazy; they had tended his wounds.

"But they wouldn't help me. They wouldn't even look in the records to prove my innocence. A mistake. A fault in the matter transmitter, and I am condemned because of it."

He looked at the bloodstained bandages, and something hurt in his head.

"Now I'll never get home to my wife," he sobbed.

➤ THE LIFE PRESERVERS

RUBBLE AND DIRT had once been piled high to cover the object, then the resulting mound had been hidden beneath a stone cairn. Either the stones had been badly fitted together or the seasons had been most unkind, because the cairn was now only a tumbled ruin, an ugly jumble of rocks no higher than a man's waist. The rubble and dirt had been washed away by the rains of centuries so that now, rising from a foliage-covered hillock, there stood the object that great labor had worked to conceal: a giant frame of pitted, corroded metal three meters high and twice as long. Set into this frame was what appeared to be a slab of slatelike material. It was hard, it had not been scratched or dented at all during the long years, and was coated with dust and adhesive debris. Around the tumbled stones and the framed slab stretched a tufted meadow bordered by a growth of stunted trees. Drab hills were visible in the distance, barely seen through a thin mist, merging into a sky of the same indifferent color. The white spheres of a recent hail shower lay unmelted in the hollows. A bird, brown on the back and light gray below, pecked desultorily at the grasses on the mound.

The change was abrupt. In an instant, too small a measure of time to be seen, the framed slab changed color. It was now a deep black, a strange color that was more lack of color than anything else. At the same moment its surface must have altered because all of the dust and debris fell from it. A detached cocoon from some large insect dropped next to the bird, so that it flew away in a sudden flurry of motion.

From the blackness a man emerged, stepping out, three-dimensional and sound, as though he were stepping through a door. He emerged, suddenly, and crouched low, looked about suspiciously. He wore a sealed suit to which were attached many complex devices. His head was contained in a transparent helmet and he held a pistol ready in his hand. After a moment he straightened up, still alert, and spoke into the microphone fixed before his lips. A length of flexible wire ran from the microphone, through a fixture in his helmet, and back to the black surface into which it vanished.

"First report. Nothing moving, no one in sight. Thought I saw something like a bird then, can't be sure. Must be winter or a cold planet, small growths and trees, low clouds, snow—no, I think it's hail—on the ground. All instruments recording well. I'm going to look at the controls now. They are concealed behind a mound of soil and rocks; I'll have to dig down for them.''

After a last searching glance around, he slipped his weapon back into its holster on his leg then took a rodlike instrument from his pack. He held it at arm's length, switched it on, and touched it to the ground where it covered the right-hand side of the frame. The soil stirred, boiling away in a cloud of fine particles, while pebbles and small stones bounced in all directions. With greater effort larger stones were moved, grating and crashing to one side when the metal tip was placed beneath them. More and more of the metal frame was revealed. It widened out below the ground and appeared to be marred by a gaping opening. The man stopped suddenly when he saw this and, after another searching look in all directions, he bent down for a closer examination.

"Reason enough here, looks like deliberate sabotage. Warped edges to the hole, an explosion, powerful. Blew out all the controls and deactivated the screen. I can fix a unit—''

His words ended in a grunt of pain as the short wooden shaft penetrated his back. It was feathered and notched. He dropped to his knees and turned about, painfully yet still quickly, and his pistol spat out a continuous stream of small particles that exploded with surprising power when they contacted anything. He laid down this curtain of fire twenty meters away, an arc of explosions and dust and smoke. There was something pressing up against the fabric of his suit over his chest and when he touched it with his fingertips he could feel a sharp point just emerging from his flesh. He was also aware of the seep of blood against his skin. As soon as the arc of explosions had cut a 180-degree swath he stood, stumbled, and half fell against the darkness from which he had emerged. He vanished into it as though into a pool of water and was gone.

A thin cold wind dispersed the dust and everything was silent once again.

The destroyed village was a place of revolting death. As always reality went far beyond imagination, and no director would have set his stage so clumsily. Untouched houses stood among the burnt ones. A draft animal lay dead between the poles of a farm wagon, its outstretched nose touching the face of a plague victim whose limbs had been gnawed by wild animals. There were other corpses tumbled clumsily about, and undoubtedly more of them mercifully out of sight inside the buildings. An arm hung down from behind the partially closed blinds of a window, a mute indication of what lay within. The projected scene was three dimensional, filling one entire wall of the darkened auditorium, real enough to shock. Which was its purpose. The commentator's voice was flat and emotionless, counterpoint to the horrors of the scene.

"Of course this occurred during the early founding days and our forces were spread thin. Notification was received and registered, but because of the deteriorating situation on Lloyd no teams were dispatched. Subsequent analysis proved that a single unit could have been spared without altering the Lloyd effort in any measurable manner, and this action would have altered drastically the results seen here. The death figures, as they stood at the end of the emergency, reached seventy-six point thirty-two of the planetary population. . . ."

The communicator in Jan Dacosta's pocket hummed quietly and he placed it to his ear and actuated it.

"Doctor Dacosta, please report to Briefing Central."

He almost jumped to his feet, despite the past weeks of training. But he controlled himself, stood slowly, then left the auditorium with no evidence of haste. A few people looked up to watch him go, then turned back to the training film. Jan had seen enough training films. Perhaps this call from Briefing meant that a mission was finally going out, that he could do something at last rather than look on, impotently, at more films. He was on alert standby, had been for days. This *could* be a mission. Once in the hallway, with no one in sight, he walked much faster. When he turned a corner he saw a familiar figure hobbling ahead of him and he hurried to catch up.

"Dr. Toledano," he called out, and the old man looked about, then stopped to wait for him.

"A mission," he said as Jan came up, speaking the language of their home world rather than the usual Inter. He smiled, his dark, wrinkled features very much like a withered plum. Jan put his hand out without thinking, and the older doctor seized it with both of his. Toledano was a tiny man, barely coming up to Jan's chest, but there was an air of surety about him that denied his size.

"I am taking this one out," he said. "Perhaps my last one. I have had enough field work. I want

you as my assistant. Three other doctors, all senior
to you. You won't have any freedom or command.
But you will learn. Agreed?''

"I couldn't ask for more, Doctor."

"Agreed then." Dr. Toledano withdrew his hands
and the smile. The air of friendliness was gone,
wiped away in an instant. "It will be hard work
and you will get little credit for it. But you will
learn."

"That's all I want, Doctor."

The friendship was also gone, packed away in
its right place until the time when it could be taken
out again. They were from the same planet, they
had friends in common. This had absolutely nothing to do with their professional relationship. Walking one step to the rear, Jan followed Toledano
into Briefing Central where the other doctors were
already waiting. They stood when the senior doctor entered.

"Take your seats, please. I believe that there is
one introduction that must be made. This gentle-
man is Dr. Dacosta, who is a recent arrival. He is
beginning his training for a permanent staff position in EPC. Since he is a qualified physician he
will accompany us on this mission as my personal
assistant, responsible to me and outside of the
regular chain of command." Then the others were
introduced, one at a time.

"Dr. Dacosta, I want you to know that these are
the important people. The entire mission is designed to get these specialists to the new planet
safely so they can do their surveys. I begin with
the lady, Dr. Bucuros, our microbiologist."

She nodded briefly, gray-haired and square-faced,

her fingers tapping lightly on the tabletop. She wanted to get on with the work.

"Dr. Oglasiti, virologist. You undoubtedly know his work and must have used his text in school."

The olive-skinned man smiled quickly and warmly, a brief flash of even white teeth. The tall, blond, almost albino man sitting next to him nodded when he was introduced in turn.

"And Dr. Pidik, epidemiologist. The one we hope will have no work to do at all."

All of them, except the still grim Dr. Bucuros, smiled at this sally, though the good humor faded instantly when Toledano opened the folder of papers on the table before him. He sat at the head of the conference table, next to the transparent wall that divided the room in two.

"This is going to be a long session," Toledano said. "We have a no-contact that the techs say approaches a thousand years." He waited, frowning slightly, until the hum of excitement had passed. "This is something of a record so we are going to have to prepare for almost any contingency. I want you to hear the scout's report. We have little more than that to go on." He pressed one of the controls on the table before him.

A door opened on the far side of the dividing wall and a man walked in slowly and sat in the chair next to the barrier, just a few feet away from them. He wore the green of an MT scout, although his collar was open and white bandages could be seen inside. His right arm was in a sling. He looked very tired and did not move when he was addressed.

"I am Dr. Toledano in charge of the mission.

These are the doctors on my team. We would like to hear your report.''

"Scout Starke, Senior Grade."

They heard his words clearly, the concealed microphones and loudspeakers took care of that. This movement of electrons was the only connection between the two sides of the room—between the two separate and completely self-contained parts of the EPC Center. Starke was no longer biologically uncontaminated so he was now in quarantine in beta section, the "dirty" side of the center. The clean, the alpha side, was as biologically sterile as was possible.

"Scout Starke," Dr. Toledano said, looking at a sheaf of papers in his hand, "I want you to tell us what happened to you personally, on this planet. The instrumentation report reveals that the planet is habitable, oxygen, temperature, pollutants all within the normal range of adaptability. Can you add anything to that? I understand the transmatter was activated using the new Y-rider reversal effect?"

"Yes, sir. There have been less than a dozen transmatters activated in this way. The process is expensive and very delicate. All of the other transmatters were either on the league planets or in uninhabitable locations—"

"Pardon me," Jan interrupted, then hurried on, very aware of the sudden attention of the others. "I'm afraid I don't know anything about this Y-rider reversal effect."

"It is in your briefing manual," Dr. Toledano said, his voice emotionless. "In the fine print in the rear. You should have seen it. It is a technique by which contact can be established with a trans-matter even if its controls are turned off or useless.''

Jan looked at his hands, aware that the others were smiling at him and not wanting to see their faces. He had meant to read all the technical reports, but there had been so little time.

"Please continue, Scout."

"Yes, sir. The transmatter was activated and showed adequate pressure, temperature, and gravity on the other side. So I went through. First contact is always made as quickly as possible after activation. A bleak landscape, cold—my impressions are in the report—felt like winter. No one in sight. The transmatter was half buried. Looked as though it had been covered at one time. I dug down to the controls and saw that they had been blasted away."

"You are sure of that?"

"Positive. Typical explosive flanges. There are photographs. I was attaching a new control unit when I was shot with an arrow. I withdrew. I saw no one and have no idea who shot me."

Further questioning elicited no more information from the scout and he was dismissed. Toledano put a block of plastic down before them into which was sealed the unsterile arrow. They examined it with interest.

"Doesn't seem quite right," Oglasiti said. "The wrong length perhaps, too short."

"You are perfectly correct," Toledano said, tapping one of the papers on the table before him. "The historical section agrees that it was not fired from the normal flexed bow we are familiar with from sporting events, but from an ancient variant called a crossbow. There are diagrams here and details of the construction and operation. This form of arrow is called a quarrel. It is well made and finished and carefully balanced. The head is made of cast iron. In their opinion, if this reflects the most advanced artifacts on the planet, the culture is early iron age.''

"Retrogrades!"

"Correct. Examination of the photographs reveals that the transmatter is at least a thousand years old, one of the original planet-openers. Considering the level of the culture we can assume that this is the only transmatter on the planet and that they have been out of communication with the rest of the galaxy since soon after the settlement. They are certainly retrogrades. Their culture has slid back to whatever level they were capable of sustaining on their own. We may never find out why the transmatter controls were destroyed. But that becomes academic at this point. Those thousand years of no-contact are our biggest concern.''

"Mutation, adaptation, and variation," Dr. Bucuros said, speaking for all of them.

"That is our problem. There are people alive on the planet, which means they have adapted successfully. There will have been local diseases and infections which they have survived, and now have resistance to, which we might find deadly. They may have no resistance at all to diseases we find commonplace. Gentlemen—and Dr. Bucuros —at this point I will make my set speech about the history of the EPC. We are so used to the initials that we tend to forget that they stand for Emergency Plague Control. This organization was founded in an emergency and exists to prevent another emergency. The plague years came roughly two hundred years after the widespread use of matter transmission. Some attempts to control the spread of disease had always been made, but they were not adequate. Because of the basic differences in planetary metabolism and philogeny almost no diseases were found that could affect mankind. But our own viruses and bacilli mutated in the very different environments they were exposed to and this proved to be the big danger. At first there were disease pockets that quickly grew to plagues. Entire populations were wiped out. The EPC was formed to combat this danger, with all planetary governments contributing equally to its support. After the control of the plagues, and the terrible losses incurred, the EPC was continued as being essential in preventing another outbreak. There are permanent members, like myself and Dr. Dacosta, and assigned specialists, like yourselves, who serve a tour of duty with us. We are involved in prevention, and will do anything to prevent a recurrence of the plague years. I stress the word *anything* because I mean anything. We are plague preventers first, physicians second. We protect the galaxy, not a single individual or planet. This retrograde planet poses—potentially—the biggest threat I have known during my entire career. We must see to it that it stays just a threat, nothing more than that.

"I will now outline my arrangements for the operation."

*   *   *

It was an hour before dawn when the light tank
erupted from the transmatter screen. The treads
tore at the hard soil and its transmission whined
loudly in the silence. At apparently foolhardy speed
it roared across the rutted ground in absolute darkness, heading toward the nearest high piece of
ground.

The driver sat calmly at the controls, his face
pressed to the optical headpiece. Infrared headlights washed the terrain ahead with invisible
radiation—clearly visible to him through the lenses.
When he topped the rise he spun the tank in a
circle, examining the area all around him, before
turning off the engines.

"All clear visibly. You can put up the detector
now."

His companion nodded and actuated the controls. A heat shield unfolded on top of the tank—to
cancel out the radiation from the tank below—and
the scanning head began to rotate. The operator
watched the display on the screen before him for a
moment before switching on the radio.

"Positioned on highest point two hundred meters from screen. Detector now operating. Numerous small heat sources undoubtedly local animal
life. Two larger sources, estimated distance ninety-
five meters, now moving away from this position.
Large animals or human beings. Since they remain
close together and seem to be traveling in a direct
line estimate they are human. No other sources
within range. End transmission."

A second tank had emerged from the screen and
was stationed in front of it. It relayed the message

to the waiting convoy, then moved aside as they emerged.

They made an impressive sight. Fourteen vehicles in all—scout tanks, armored troop carriers, supply trucks, trailers. Their large headlights cut burning arcs across the landscape, and as each one emerged the roar of motors and transmissions grew louder. The command car pulled up next to the scout tank and Dr. Toledano stood on a specially elevated step to survey the landscape. There was a growing band of light on one horizon, what they would now call the east.

"Anything more on the detector?" he asked Jan, who sat below operating the radio liaison.

"Negative. The first two blips have moved off the screen."

"Then we'll hold here until it gets light. Keep the detector going and keep everyone alert. When we can drive without lights we'll move out in the direction those blips took."

It was a short wait. Dawn came with surprising suddenness—they must be near the equator—and the first rays of reddish sunlight threw long shadows across the landscape.

"Move out," Toledano ordered. "Single column, guide on me. Scouts out on both flanks and point. I want some prisoners. Use gas, I don't want any casualties."

Jan Dacosta relayed the message evenly, though he felt certain internal misgivings. He was a doctor, a physician, and the role he was playing now felt more than a little strange. The operation seemed more military than medical so far. He shrugged aside his doubts. Toledano knew what he was doing. The best thing that he could do was watch and learn.

The convoy moved out. Within a few minutes the scout tank on point reported habitation ahead and halted until the others caught up. Jan joined Toledano in the open turret when they stopped on the ridge above the valley, next to the scout tank.

"It's like something out of a history book," Jan said.

"Very rare. The cultural anthropologists and technological historians will have a field day here once we open the planet up."

Morning mist still lay in the valley below, drifting up from the river that snaked by in a slow curve. Plowed fields surrounded a village, a small town really, that huddled on the riverbank. Roofs could be seen, jammed closely together, with the thin ribbons of smoke rising up from the morning fires. The houses were pressed close together because the entire settlement was surrounded by a high stone wall, complete with towers, arrow slits, a sealed gate—and all encompassed by a water-filled moat. Not a soul was in sight and if it had not been for the streamers of smoke it could have been a city of the dead.

"Locked up and sealed," Jan said. "They must have heard us coming."

"It would have taken a deaf man not to."

The radio beeped and Jan answered it. "One of the flankers, Doctor. They have a prisoner."

"Fine. Get him here."

The tank rumbled up brief minutes later and the prisoner was handed down, strapped to an evacuation stretcher. The circle of waiting doctors looked on with unconcealed interest as the stretcher was placed on the ground before them.

The man appeared to be in his middle fifties, gray-bearded and lank-haired. He lay with his mouth open, snoring deeply, rendered instantly unconscious by the sleepgas capsules. The few teeth visible were blackened stumps. His clothing consisted of a heavy, sleeveless leather poncho, worn over roughspun woolen breeks and shirt. The thick leather, knee-high boots had wooden soles fastened to them. Neither clothing nor boots were very clean and there was ingrained dirt in the creases of his limp hands.

"Obtain your specimens before we waken him," Toledano ordered, and the technicians carried over the equipment.

The doctors were efficient and quick. Blood samples were taken, as well as skin scrapings, hair and nail cuttings, sputum samples, and, after a great deal of working at the thick clothing, a spinal tap. More specimens for biopsy would be obtained later, but this would be a good beginning. Dr. Bucuros exclaimed happily as she routed out and captured some body lice.

"Excellent," Toledano said as the scientists hurried off to their laboratories. "Now wake him up and get the language technician to work. We can't do a thing until we can communicate with these people."

Burly soldiers stood by as the prisoner was awakened. Seconds after the injection his eyes fluttered and opened; he looked about in stark terror.

"Easy, easy," the language specialist said, holding out his microphone and adjusting the phone in his ear. Trailing cables led from these, and from the control box on his waist, to the computer trailer. He smiled and squatted down next to the prisoner, who was now sitting up and searching wildly in all directions for some avenue of escape.

"Talk, speak, *parla, taller, mluviti, beszelni*—"

"*Jaungoiko!*" the man shouted, starting to rise. One of the soldiers pressed him back to the stretcher. "*Diabru,*" he moaned, covering his eyes with his hands and rocking back and forth.

"Very good," the specialist said. "I have a tentative identification already. All languages fit into different linguistic families, and every word of every language and dialect is in the computer's memory banks. It needs just a few words to identify cognates and group, then it narrows down even more by supplying key words. Here comes one now." He mouthed the sounds to himself, then spoke aloud.

"*Nor?*"

"*Zer?*" The prisoner answered, uncovering his eyes.

"*Nor . . . zu . . . itz egin.*"

The process continued rapidly after that. The more words the prisoner spoke the more referents the computer had. Once the language group was known it had this stock of roots to draw on and then proceeded to determine the variations from the norm. Within a half an hour the specialist stood up and brushed off his knees.

"Communication established, sir. Have you used this unit before?"

"The Mark-IV," Toledano said.

"This is the sixth. There have been improvements but not any operating changes. Just press the activate button on the mike when you want a translation. The computer will speak to the prisoner in his own language. Anything that he says will be translated for you.''

Toledano put on the earphone while the soldiers hung the microphone about the prisoner's neck and positioned the loudspeaker before him.

''What is your name?'' Toledano asked. A fraction of a second after he spoke, his translated question sounded from the speaker in front of the prisoner, who gaped at it in a blend of confusion and horror. Toledano repeated the question.

''Txakur,'' the man finally stammered.

''And the name of the town over there?''

The questioning progressed in fits and starts. Some questions the man could or would not answer, either through lack of knowledge or imperfect translation. The former was probably true since the computer perfected its knowledge of the language with every phrase the man spoke. Toledano seemed satisfied with the results in any case.

''The military move out in fifteen minutes,'' he told Jan. ''But I want one squad to stay behind to protect the ancillary units. Would you tell the doctors I want to see them now.''

They straggled up one by one, not happy about being taken away from their tests, but knowing better than to make any protests. Toledano waited until they were all assembled before he began.

''We have obtained some knowledge from the informant. The town over there is named Uri, as is the land about here. I imagine it is a city-state, a primitive political unit. There is another city or country called Gudaegin which seems to be in control of Uri right now. I am guessing that they have been invaded and occupied. We will find out soon enough. The Gudaegin are very warlike, the informant seems very afraid of them, and they have weapons of many kinds. They know that we are here. A warning was sent out to come to the city, and our informant was on the way there when he was captured. I am going to enter the city now and talk to the leaders. I will call you to join us when they are pacified. Meanwhile continue with your work since I will want at least preliminary reports by this evening.''

The small convoy moved off behind the command car. A rutted farm track snaked through the fields and they followed that to the brink of the moat. Two rows of piles reached from the shore to the heavy sealed gate in the town wall.

"Annoying," Toledano said, looking through the tank's periscope. "They have taken up the flooring of the causeway. We are going to have to find another way in."

Something hit the water before them, sending up a spout of water. An instant later there was a shattering clang on the tank's deck armor. Through a gunnery slit Jan had a quick glimpse of a black object dropping heavily to the ground.

"It looks like a large stone, sir."

"It does indeed. A powerful launcher of some kind. Zeroed in well. We shall have to take precautions. We will pull back fifty meters and spread out in line. Divide their fire. Then see what kind of a bottom this channel has."

It was mud, soft mud. The fire died as they

pulled back, then concentrated on the single troop carrier that rumbled back to the moat, over the edge, and down into it. The tank was completely watertight, although it never submerged all the way. But when it was only a third of the way across it stuck, treads churning uselessly, sinking deeper. Toledano had foresightedly had a heavy cable fixed to a cleat in the vehicle's rear, so it was dragged unceremoniously backward to solid ground. Small figures were visible on the wall above jumping and waving their hands.

"Enough experimentation," Toledano said. "All vehicles forward to the water's edge. Someone will have to get hurt now and I would prefer it not be us. Hook this circuit through to the computer."

"Couldn't we use sleepgas?" Jan asked. "Men in suits could swim over there and secure the place, open the gate."

"We could. But we would have casualties. We cannot saturate that place with enough gas to knock them all out without overdosing and killing a good number of them. They will have to surrender." He spoke into the microphone and his translated words boomed from the loudspeaker on the hull.

"I talk to the Gudaegin in the city of Uri. We do not wish to harm anyone. We wish to talk to you. We wish to be friends."

More rocks crashed down on the row of armored vehicles and a thick, two-meter long spear buried itself in the ground next to the tank.

"Their answer is clear enough. In their position I would probably do the same thing myself. Now let us see if we can change their minds." He switched on the microphone. "For your own safety

I ask you not to resist our entering the city. We will destroy you if we must. I ask you to leave the turret above the gate. The high turret above the gateway. Leave it now. The turret will now be destroyed to show you the power of our weapons.''

Toledano waited a few moments then issued orders to the heavy tank. "One round, high explosive. I want it taken off with the first shot. Fire."

It was massive overkill. The turret and a great bite of wall vanished in the explosion. Pieces of masonry—and bodies—wheeled high and splashed into the moat. Jan's fists were clenched, his nails digging into his palms.

"Good God, sir. Those were people. Men. You've killed them—" He choked into silence as Dr. Toledano turned and looked at him in cold anger. The translator was switched on again.

"You will now open the gate and permit us to enter. You will wave a white flag as a symbol of your agreement. If you do not the gate will be destroyed as was the turret."

The answer was a concentration of fire on the command car. Rocks slammed into it, numbing their ears and bouncing the armored car on its springs. The large metal-tipped spears clanged off its hull and a sudden thicket of their slim trunks sprang up around the car.

"Use your light cannon, gunner. I don't want the whole thing down in rubble. Just blow open the gate."

The gun fired, round after slow round. Chewing away the iron-bound planks, dropping them into wreckage and destroying the wreckage.

"There is something happening, sir—"

"Cease fire."

"There, look, on the wall! They are milling about, seem to be fighting with each other."

It was true. First one body, then another, cart-wheeled down from the wall to splash into the moat. A few moments later a length of gray cloth—it might generously be considered off-white—unrolled down the wall from the parapet above.

"Battle over," Toledano said, with no satisfaction. "They will rebuild the causeway so we can drive in, protected. I want no more deaths."

His name was Jostun and the computer translated his title as either village elder or council member. He was middle-aged and fat, but the sword he held was bloody. He stood in the middle of the rubble-filled square and waved its point at the building on the other side.

"Destroy it," he shouted. "With your explosions. Bring it down. The Gudaegin will die and the fiend of all of them, Azpi-oyal will die. You are our saviours. Do it!"

"No." Dr. Toledano snapped the answer, a flat, hard statement, understandable even before the computer could translate it. He stood alone, facing Jostun, so small he only came up to the other man's chest. But his command was undeniable. "You will join the others on the far side of the square. You will do it now."

"But we fought them for you. Helped you to win the city. We attacked the invaders by surprise and killed many of them. The survivors cower there. Kill—"

"The killing is over. This is now a time of peace. Go."

Jostun raised his hands to the sky, seeking a justice there that was being denied him here. Then he saw the waiting tanks again and he slumped, the sword dropping from his fingers, ringing on the flags. He went to the others. Toledano turned up the power on the amplifier and faced the sealed building.

"You have nothing to fear from me. Or from the people of this city. You know that I can destroy all of you in there. Now I ask you to come out and surrender and you have my promise you will not be harmed. Come out now."

As if to punctuate his words the large tank grated in a half circle on locked tread to point the gaping muzzle of its gun at the building. There was silence then, even the people of Uri were hushed and expectant, and the front door of the building squealed and opened. A man stepped out, tall, haughty, and alone. He wore a shining breastplate and helm, a sword held loosely at his side.

"Azpi-oyal!" a woman screamed, and the crowd stirred. Someone pushed through, leveling a taut crossbow. But the soldiers were ready. Gas grenades burst about the bowman and hid him from view. The bolt from the crossbow hurtled out, badly aimed, clattering from the stones of the square and slithering across almost to Azpi-oyal's feet. He ignored it and walked forward. The crowd moved back. He came up to Toledano, a muscular, dark-skinned man with a great black beard. Under the edge of his helm his eyes were cold.

"Give me your sword," Toledano said.

"Why? What will you do with me and my men? We may still die with honor like Gudaegin."

"You have no need to. No one will be harmed. Any who wish to leave may. We have made peace here and we will keep the peace."

"This was my city. When you attacked, these animals rebelled and took it from me. Will you return it to me?"

Toledano smiled coldly, admiring the man's hard nerve.

"I will not. It was not yours in the first place. It has now been returned to the people who live here."

"Where do you come from, little man, and what are you doing here? Do you dispute the right of the Gudaegin to the three continents? If you do you will never rest until you have killed us all. This city is one thing, our land is another."

"I want nothing that you have. Your lands or your fortunes. Nothing. We are here to make the sick well. We are here to show you how to contact other places, other worlds. We are here to change things, but change them only to make them better. Nothing that you value will be changed in any way."

Azpi-oyal weighed his sword in his hand and thought. He was not a stupid man. "We value the strength of our arms and our people. We mean to rule on the three continents. Will you take away our conquests?"

"Your past ones, no. But you will have no future ones. We cure disease and your kind of killing can be a disease. You will have to give it up. You will soon find that you do not miss it. As a first step on that road you will give me your sword." Toledano put out his tiny, almost child-size hand.

Azpi-oyal stepped back in anger, clutching the pommel. The turret on a tank squealed as it turned to follow him. He looked with hatred at the lowered muzzles of the guns—then burst out laughing. Tossing the sword into the air he caught it by the point and extended it to Toledano.

"I don't know whether to believe you or not, small conqueror. But I think I would like to live a little longer to see what you are going to do to the three continents. A man may always die."

The worst was over. Politically at least. They would now have a period of relative peace during which the tests and examinations could be made. A thousand years of isolation was a long time.

"We must get started," Toledano said, with sudden irritation, as he waved the radio operator to him. "Enough time has been wasted. Have the other units move up. We'll set up a base in this square here."

"The line is longer if anything," Jan said, looking out of the window. "Must be a hundred or more. It looks like the word has finally gotten out that we aren't doing terrible things to the citizens here, but are actually curing some of their ills."

They had occupied a large warehouse near the main gate and a medical aid station had been set up. There had been few volunteers for their glittering and exotic instruments at first, but they had enough involuntary patients among the wounded survivors of the fighting. Most of these had already been given up for dead. The crude local knowledge of medicine did not appear to go beyond bone setting, suturing of simple wounds, and amputation. The notion of antisepsis had stayed with them through the lost centuries, and they used alcohol as an antiseptic and boiled the bandages and instruments. But they had no way of treating infections—other than by amputation—so that death was the usual result of any deep, puncturing wound. The doctors had changed all that. None of their patients died. They healed abdominal wounds, repaired shattered limbs and heads, cured gangrene and other major infections, and even sewed back on a severed arm. This last seemed more miraculous than medical and soon the townspeople were flocking for treatment with almost religious enthusiasm.

"The waste, the absolute waste," Dr. Pidik said, giving the patient before him, a frightened girl, an injection of fungicide. "War first, that's where all the talent and energy goes, with medical care lagging ages behind. They have engineers, mechanics, builders. Did you see those steam ballistae? A pressure tank and miles of pipe and those piston-actuated things that dropped rocks right down the exhaust pipes of the tanks. You might think they could spare a miniscule amount of energy for some work on the healing arts."

The tall epidemiologist bent his blond head low, carefully cutting away dead tissue and swabbing out the wounds on the girl's monstrously swollen foot. It was twice its normal size, dark, knobby, decayed. There was no pain, the local anaesthetic took care of that, yet she was still terrified at what was happening.

"I've never seen anything like that at all," Jan said. "I don't believe there is even a reference in our text books."

"This is one of the diseases of neglect; you'll find it mentioned in the older texts. You'll see many things like this in the backwaters of the galaxy. It's maduromycosis. There is first a penetrating wound, common enough, that plants fungus spores deep inside the flesh. If untreated this is the result after a course of years."

"I've seen this, though," Jan said, taking the hand of the blank-eyed man who had been led before him. He rotated the man's hand in a circle, then let go of it. The rotation of the hand continued, automatically, as though a machine had been set into motion. "Echopraxis, meaningless repetition of motions once they are started."

Pidik looked up and snorted. "Yes, I imagine you have seen it. But you found it in the mental wards, a condition of paranoia. I'm willing to bet this is from physical causes, untreated cranial fracture or some such."

"No bets," Jan said, touching lightly the heavily depressed area in the man's skull. It was surrounded by scar tissue and obviously an old wound.

They had a little of everything. Infections, sores, diseases, chronic illnesses, carcinomas. Everything. It was nearly dusk when Pidik called a halt.

"Almost twelve standard hours at this. Enough. They can come back tomorrow. This planet has too long a period of rotation and it takes some getting used to."

Jan repeated the order through the computer and, after not too many complaints, the patients allowed themselves to be pushed out by the guards. All but the sickest stayed in their positions in line, huddling against the wall, to be treated the following day. Jan joined Pidik at the sink where he was washing up.

"I can't thank you too much, Dr. Pidik. Since you have been helping me I think we have seen ten times as many patients. There are so many things here I know nothing about. There really should be a medical school for EPC physicians."

"There is. Right here in the field. You have had good training. There is nothing here you can't treat after some experience. And Dr. Toledano will see that you get it."

"Isn't this taking you from your work?"

"This is my work. An epidemiologist is no good without an epidemic. I've looked at all the samples and seen the various kinds of wildlife these people carry in their bloodstreams. Nothing exotic so far, nothing alien. Just a good selection of the bacilli and viruses and such that have dwelt in mankind since the beginning of time. Here in the field I may see something that we have missed in the labs."

Jan shook the water from his hands and took a towel. "We've been here almost a month," he said. "If there were any exotic infections wouldn't we have turned them up by now?"

"Not necessarily. We've only been looking at one corner of an entire world. Once our in-depth study is made here we can do a more general survey of the rest of the planet. When it has been cleared for contact the politicians and the traders will come through."

"Do you believe Azpi-oyal's story that an entire army of Gudaegin is on the way?"

"Absolutely. His people seem to have conquered almost all of the other groups on this planet. They won't stand for us taking away one of their cities. But Dr. Toledano will be able to handle them—"

"Some kind of a riot developing, Doctors," a sergeant said, poking his head into the room. "And it seems to be about some kind of sickness. Could we have your help?"

"I'll come," Jan said, swinging the communicator to his shoulder.

"So will I," Pidik said. "I don't like the sound of this."

A squad of soldiers was waiting for them outside, weapons at the port. The sergeant led. Before they had gone more than a few paces they could hear the distant roar of voices. As they came closer individual screams and cries rose above the continual shouting, and then the thud of exploding gas grenades. They double-timed the rest of the way.

Only the guns of the soldiers and the waiting tank kept the hysterical mob from attacking. A huddle of unconscious bodies proved that even this had not been enough. As they pushed through to the line of defenders in front of the building, Dr. Pidik waved the sergeant to him.

"The computer can't make any sense out of this noise. Grab someone who looks like a spokesman and get him over here."

There was a sudden bustle of action and the

sergeant reappeared, half dragging a burly citizen of Uri who was still a little dazed by the sergeant's efficient means of argument. He was a tall man with a broad chest, sporting a scraggle of beard and a patch over one eye. The other, red and malevolent, peered from beneath a jutting brow ridge.

"What is wrong? Why are you all here?" Pidik asked the man through the computer's translation unit.

"The plague! They have the plague in there. Burn down the house and kill all in it. That's what you do with the plague. Death cures!"

"It's the final cure," Pidik said calmly. "But let us see if there aren't other not quite so drastic measures that we can use first. Come on," he said to Jan, and started up the stairs toward the house.

A moan rose up when the crowd saw what they were doing, followed by an even more intense howl of anger. Despite the guards the mob pressed forward.

"Use gas if you must," Pidik ordered. "But stop them right here."

Clouds of vapor sprung up as he hammered on the door and called through the translator for them to open it. It remained sealed and silent.

"Open this," Pidik ordered the nearest soldier.

The man eyed the tall door and noticed the boltheads for the hinges on one side. He pressed small explosive charges over these spots, close to the frame, pushed in timers, and stepped back.

"Ten seconds, sir. They're shaped charges, punch right through, but there can be a certain amount of reverse blast."

They hugged the wall as the sharp crack of the double explosion sounded. The crowd wailed. The two doctors climbed over the ruined door and followed the sound of running feet through a dark hallway. At the end, with the last rays of sunlight filtering through a high, barred window, they found a man lying in bed. A huddle of women and children were pressed silently into the corner.

"Corporal," Pidik said to the soldier who had followed them in. "Get these people out of here. See that no one else enters the building. Call Dr. Toledano for more aid if you need it."

"We'll hold them fine, sir, not to worry."

"Very good. Give me your light then before you go."

The intense beam shot out and the man on the bed moaned, turning his head away and shielding his eyes with his arm. The inside of his forearm was swollen and red, covered with tiny pustules. Dr. Pidik took the man's hand, frowning as he felt the fever-heat of the skin, and gently pulled his arm away from his face. The man's features were also red and swollen, his eyes almost closed, and at first they did not recognize him.

"It's Jostun," Jan said. "The council leader."

"*Izuri* . . ." Jostun muttered, thrashing back and forth on the pillow.

"Plague," Pidik said. "That word is clear enough. Get an ambulance here at once and pass word that I want to use the isolation ward. And tell Dr. Toledano what is happening so he can alert the troops."

Jostun called out to them, and Pidik held out the translator microphone.

"Leave me . . . burn the building. . . . I am dead. It is the plague."

"We are going to take care of you—"

"Death alone cures the plague!" Jostun shouted, half rising as he did so, then falling back heavily, moaning with the effort.

"They all seem pretty convinced of that," Jan said.

"Well I'm not. A disease is a disease—and has a cure. Now let's get him moved."

The city was in a panic. The ambulance had to drive slowly through the dark streets to avoid running over the limp bodies that were strewn on all sides. Sleepgas was being used in greater and greater quantities by the outnumbered soldiers. The encampment in the square was a besieged lager whose defenders opened a gate in the perimeter to admit the ambulance.

"What is the disease?" Toledano said, appearing as the stretcher was carried into the hospital.

"I am sure that I don't know yet, Doctor. I will inform you when I do."

"I suggest it be quick. We have seven other cases already."

Pidik turned away without another word and Toledano beckoned to Jan. "Come with me." He started at a fast walk toward his headquarters prefab with Jan hurrying after him. They reached it just as a troop carrier slid to a stop and an officer jumped down.

"Bad news, sir. One of the wall positions was attacked, both men dead. The alarm went off and we fought our way back there, but . . ." He hesitated. "We think they got someone over the wall. This is the man who was in charge."

A limp figure was carried out and dropped, not too gently, at their feet. Toledano looked at the slack features and grunted. "Aspi-oyal; I might have known. Bring him into my office. Jan, wake him up."

Inside, in the brilliantly lit room, the reddish flush on Azpi-oyal's skin was clearly seen, and when Jan gave him the injection the skin was hot to his touch.

"I'm afraid that he has it too, sir," Jan said.

Azpi-oyal blinked back to consciousness, straightened up and smiled. There was no trace of warmth in the smile.

"My messenger has gone," he said into the translator. "You will not be able to stop him."

"I would not want to. I see no reason why you should not contact your own people. Your army must not be more than a day's march away."

Azpi-oyal started slightly at this mention. "Since you know about the Gudaegin, fifty thousand strong, you will know that you are lost. I have sent them the message to come here, and to destroy this city and all who dwell within it. Now tell me that you would have permitted that message to be sent?"

"Of course I would," Toledano said calmly. "This will not be done. The city will stand and all will live."

"The plague sufferers—like myself—will be killed. The plague bearers, yourselves, will be destroyed."

"Not at all." Toledano sat down and put the back of his hand to his mouth while he yawned.

"We did not bring the plague. But we shall destroy the plague and cure all who suffer from it. You will now be taken to a place where you can rest." He called the guards and switched off the translator. He still spoke calmly, but there was an urgency now to the meaning of his words.

"Take this man to the hospital and see that he is well treated but under constant guard. Use as many men as necessary. He is not to be left unwatched at any time nor is he to escape. This is vital. Do you understand?"

"Yes, sir."

"Might I ask what is happening?" Jan said when they had gone.

"Scouts reported this Gudaegin army a few hours ago. They must not like our taking away one of their captured cities. I hoped to use Azpi-oyal to make peace with them. I still shall, if we can find a cure for this plague."

"What was this nonsense about our bringing the plague?"

"No nonsense. It looks like the truth, though I don't see how it can be. Allowing for minor variations due to incubation period, the only people who are getting sick are the ones who had first contact with us. There is no way of escaping that fact."

Jan was shocked. "It just can't be that way, sir! The only microscopic life we carry in our systems is intestinal flora. Which is harmless. Our equipment is sterile. It is impossible that we could be involved."

"Yet we are. We must now find out how—"

Dr. Pidik burst through the door and dropped a

slide on the desk. "There's your culprit," he announced. "A coccobacillary microorganism. It takes an aniline stain and is gram-negative."

"You sound like you are describing a rickettsia?" Toledano said.

"I am. Their blood is teaming with the beasts."

"Typhus?" Jan asked.

"Very much like it. A mutated strain perhaps. And I thought they were immune. We found traces of an organism like this in a number of the blood samples we took. Yet the individuals were healthy. They aren't anymore."

Toledano paced back and forth the length of the small room. "It does not make sense," he said. "Typhus and all the related diseases are vectored by insects, mites, body lice. I have complaints about the EPC, but we *couldn't* have been involved in that way. But there still appears to be a connection. Perhaps in the country through which we drove, we might have picked up something on the way. Yet there has been no sickness among our personnel. We will have to look into this. But getting a cure comes first, top priority. Cure them first and we'll find the source later."

"I have an idea about that—" Jan said, but broke off at the sound of a distant splintering crash followed by screams and shouting. At the same moment the duty lieutenant ran in.

"We're under fire, sir. Steam ballistae, bigger than anything in the city. They must have moved them up as soon as it became dark."

"Can we knock them out without hurting anyone?"

"Negative, sir. They are out of range of gas weapons. We could—"

He never finished the sentence. A crashing roar hammered at their ears, stunning them, and all the lights went out. The floor buckled and Jan found himself hurled down. As he climbed to his feet the beam of the lieutenant's light cut a dust-filled path through the darkness, moved across the sprawled forms, and came to rest on the rough slab of stone that had crashed down upon them.

"Dr. Toledano!" someone shouted, and the light came to rest, flickering erratically as though the hand that held it were shaking.

"Nothing, no hope," Pidik said, bending over the small huddled form. "It took half his head away. Dead instantly." He stood and sighed. "I have to get back to the laboratory. I imagine this means you will be taking over, Dr. Dacosta."

He was almost to the entrance before Jan could gather his wits and call after him. "Wait, what do you mean?"

"Just that. You were his assistant. You are career EPC. The rest of us have other things to do."

"He never intended—"

"He never intended to die. He was my friend. Do the sort of job he would have wanted you to do." Then he was gone.

It was too much to accept all at once, but Jan forced himself to act. The chain of command could be straightened out later. Now it was an emergency.

"Have Dr. Toledano's body removed to the hospital," he ordered the lieutenant, and waited until the command had been passed on. "I recall the last thing you said was something about their being out of the range of gas, the things that are firing at us?''

''Yes, sir, they're beyond a ridge of hills.''

''Can we locate them exactly?''

''We can. We have artillery spotters, infrared, camera equipped, miniature copters.''

''Send one out. Get the location and range of the emplacement, look for the steam generator. If this weapon is like the ones on the walls—it should be, only bigger—there will be one generator and pipes to the ballistae. Locate this and, with one gun firing, what do you call it . . . ?''

''Ranging in?''

''Exactly. When you have the range blow up the generator. That will stop the firing. You'll kill some people, but there are more being killed right here. Including Dr. Toledano.''

The officer saluted and left. Jan was suddenly tired and he went to the washroom to put cold water on his face. A brilliant emergency light came on in the room behind him and in the glass over the sink he looked into his own eyes. Had he really issued that order to kill, just like that? He had. For the greater good of course. He looked away from the mirrored eyes and plunged his face into the water.

Dawn was only a few hours away and most of those present had the drawn looks of near exhaustion. The ceiling of the office had been patched, a new desk brought in, all signs of damage removed. Jan sat behind the desk, in what had once been Dr.

Toledano's chair, and waved the others to seats as they came in.

"It looks like we are all here now," he said. "Dr. Pidik, could you give us the medical situation first?"

"Under control, I'll say that much." The tall epidemiologist rubbed at his unshaven jaw. "We haven't lost any patients yet, supportive treatment seems to be working with even the worst cases. But we can do nothing to stop the spread of the disease. It's absolutely out of control. If it continues at this rate we are going to have everyone in the city sick, we'll have to call in help to handle them. I've never seen anything like this before in my entire life."

"How does it look from the military point of view, Lieutenant?"

The officer was near the end of his strength. He lifted his hands and almost gave a shrug for an answer, controlling himself only at the last instant. He pulled himself erect. "We are having less trouble from the populace. All of our men are withdrawn from the streets, and either on the walls or guarding the camp here. A lot of people are sick, that takes the fight out of them, the rest seem sort of dazed. The enemy outside has been moving into attacking positions and I think we can expect a heavy attack at any time now, probably at dawn."

"What makes you say that?"

"The equipment they've brought up. More ballistae of all sizes. Steam-powered rams, bridging material, grappling towers. They are ready for a concerted effort and they have the men and equipment for the job."

"Can you stop the attack when it comes?"

"Not for long, sir. We might with the aid of the people in the city, but they are more than useless. We shall have to guard against them as well. There are just not enough of our troops to man the walls. If you will pardon my suggesting it, we are faced with two possible solutions. One, we can call for more troops. The technicians have set up a transmatter and a larger one can be brought through and assembled. Secondly, we can withdraw. Any defense here will be costly of men—on both sides— and equipment. The Gudaegin are tremendous fighters and never stop until they have won."

"If we leave—what happens to the people of the city?"

The lieutenant looked uncomfortable. "It's hard to say, but, I imagine, if they're sick—"

"They will all be killed. I don't think much of that as a solution, Lieutenant. And we can't take them back to base, there isn't room for a cityful of sick people. And there are no other quarantine stations that can handle them. The situation is beginning to look a little grim."

Their silence, their downcast expressions, echoed only agreement. There seemed no simple way out of the situation. A number of people were going to die no matter what they decided. These deaths would be a black mark on the record of the EPC. Perhaps another training film would be made about their mistakes, warning others not to repeat them.

"We are not beaten yet," Jan told them, when no one else elected to speak. "I have some other plans that may alter the situation. Carry on as you have been doing and by dawn I will let you know.

Lieutenant, if you would remain I would like to talk to you.''

Jan waited until the others had filed silently out and the door was closed before he spoke. "I want a volunteer, Lieutenant, a good soldier who is a professional fighting man. I am going outside of the city and I am going to need some skilled help—"

"You can't do that, sir! You're in command."

"Since I am in command there is nothing to stop me, is there? The mission I have in mind needs a young and fairly expendable medical man, for which I qualify well. The medical teams do not need me now and you can man the defenses whether I am here or not. If I get into trouble a call to headquarters can send a more highly qualified EPC man through in a few minutes. So there really is no reason why I should not go, is there?"

The lieutenant reluctantly agreed—although he did not like it—and went out in search of a volunteer. Jan was loading equipment into a pack when there was a knock on the door.

"I was told to report to you, sir," the soldier said, saluting. Jan had seen him before, a big man with a neck like a tree trunk, who nevertheless moved quickly as a cat. He was weighted with combat gear and looked ready for anything.

"What's your name?"

"Plendir, private, EPC Guard, sir."

"Weren't you wearing a sergeant's stripes a few days ago?"

"I was, sir, and not for the first time. Field demotion. Drink and fighting. Not our own men, sir. Locals. About fifteen of them jumped me. Most still in hospital, sir.''

"I hope you are as good as you say, Plendir. Ready to go with me outside of the city?''

"Yes, sir.'' His stony expression did not change.

"Good. But it's not as suicidal as it sounds. We're not going over the wall, but we'll exit by the transmatter we used when we first hit this planet. That should put us some miles behind the enemy troops. I want to capture one of them. Do you think it can be done?''

"Sounds like an interesting job, sir,'' Plendir said, almost smiling at the thought.

Jan slipped on his pack and they went to the tech section. Bright lights flooded the temporary structure while a generator whined steadily in the background, supplying the operating current for the equipment and for recharging the vehicles' high-density batteries. They stepped over cables and walked around equipment to the familiar slab shape of a personnel transmatter screen.

"Has it been checked out?'' Jan asked a passing tech.

"To the last decimal place and locked on frequency, sir.''

Jan made a note of the transmatter's code on the inside of his wrist, and Plendir automatically did the same. Until they had the call number memorized they did not want to risk being locked out of the city.

"If I might make a suggestion?'' Plendir asked, as Jan punched the code for the other transmatter on the keyboard.

"What is it?''

"We are, so to speak, going into my area of operation now. We have no idea of who or what might be waiting on the other side. I go through first and roll left. You come after me as quickly as you can and dive right. Then we are both through and down low and looking things over."

"Just as you say, Plendir. But we are far enough from the enemy troops so I don't think we have to worry."

The soldier raised his eyebrows slightly, but otherwise did not answer. When the operation light came on he waved Jan forward—then dived head-first at the screen. Jan jumped right after him, ready to hit the ground.

Cold air, black night, a sharp explosion, and something heavy hitting the ground next to him. Jan dropped, harder than he had planned, driving the air from his lungs. By the time he had gasped and lifted his head to look around the brief battle was over. A man lay on the ground near him, slumped and unconscious, and another was near the crouching Plendir, rolling and moaning softly. A cloud of gas, barely visible in the starlight, was drifting away from three other motionless figures. There was a crackling in the brush that lessened and died away.

"All clear, sir. They were on guard here, but I was maybe expecting them and they weren't expecting me. Not just then, if you know what I mean. That one by you may be dead, couldn't help it, me or him. But this one has a broken wing and the others are gassed. Will any of them do?"

"The wounded one will be best, let me look at

him." Jan stood and swung off his pack. "Some of them got away, didn't they?"

"Yes, sir. They'll be bringing back their friends. How long will you need?"

"Fifteen minutes should do it. Think we can manage that much?"

"Probably. But I'll give you all the time I can. Need help with him before I take a look around?"

"Yes, just one second."

The prisoner winced away from the harsh light. Other than his metal helm there was nothing very soldierly about him, dressed in coarse cloth and half-cured furs. He tried to scrabble away when Jan touched his arm, but the sudden appearance of the point of a trench knife just in front of his eyes changed his mind. Jan was quick. He slipped an inflatable cast over the arm, set the bones through the flexible fabric, then triggered the pressure. It blew up with a quick hiss, holding the broken arm rigid and secure.

"He's not going to like what comes next, so could you tie his wrists and ankles together and roll him onto his side."

Plendir did this with quick efficiency while Jan spread out the contents of his pack. He had blunt-tipped surgical shears that he used to cut away the prisoner's clothing. The man began to howl and Jan shut him up with a piece of sticking tape over his mouth.

"I'd like to look about, sir," Plendir said, sniffing the air. "It's going to be dawn soon."

"I'm fine here."

The soldier slipped soundlessly away and Jan balanced the light on a rock while he bared the man's not-too-clean back. There was a muffled moan. From his pack Jan took the thing he put together earlier, a great square made by criss-crossing many lengths of surgical sticking tape. He help the prisoner from moving with his knee while he slapped the square across the man's back. As Jan pressed it into place the man moaned at the cold touch and tried to shiver away. Jan stood, brushing off his knees, and looked at his watch.

Dawn was lightening the east when Plendir reappeared.

"They made good time, sir," he reported. "There must be a camp near here. Anyway a whole gang of them are on the way now."

"How long do we have?"

"Two, maybe three minutes, at the very outside."

Jan looked at his watch. "I need at least three minutes. Can you arrange some kind of holding action?"

"My pleasure," Plendir said, and went off at a trot.

They were very long minutes, with the second hand of the watch moving as though crawling through molasses. There was still a minute to go when there was the sound of distant explosions and shouts.

"Time enough," Jan said, and bent swiftly to tear off the sticking plaster. He did it with a sudden pull, but it took plenty of hair with it and the prisoner writhed in silent agony. Jan stuffed the square into his pack before permitting himself a quick flash of the light.

"Wonderful!" he shouted.

The man's back had a pattern of square red

welts, one bigger than the others and so swollen
that it projected like an immense boil from his
skin. Plendir came pelting back at a dead run.

"They're right behind me!"

"One second, I need the evidence!"

Jan fumbled out the camera as the soldier spun
about and hurled gas grenades back in the direction he had come from. The flash burst out its
sudden light and Jan shouted, "Let's go!" Something hissed by his ear.

"Do it—I'm right behind you!"

Jan hit the actuator on the preset controls and
jumped into the screen. He hit the floor, skidded
and fell as Plendir came diving through behind
him in a neat roll. The bolt from a crossbow
followed them and thunked into the wall across the
room. Plendir hit the controls and the connection
was broken.

"The last shot of the war," Jan said, smiling,
looking at the quarrel imbedded in the wall. "It
should be all over now."

The doctors looked at the blown-up print of the
color photograph, then at the square of sticking
tape that had been applied to the man's back.

"It seems obvious now by hindsight," Dr.
Bucuros reluctantly admitted, as though she were
angry she had not considered the possibility herself.

"Allergy," Dr. Pidik said. "The one thing we
never considered. But did you have to be so dramatic about obtaining a subject?"

Jan smiled. "One of the city people might have
been all right, but I couldn't be sure. I had to get
someone from outside, who had never been in

contact with us in any way. The Gudaegin soldier proved ideal as you can see. A reaction to a number of common specimens we have—and one single, massive allergic reaction right there." He tapped the photograph over the swollen red welt.

"What is the allergen?"

"Polyster. Our most common plastic. Our clothes are woven out of it, our belts, equipment parts, numberless things. It would be impossible for them *not* to come into contact with it. With disastrous results. You gave me the clue, Dr. Pidik, when you said that a lot of the people here seemed to have the inactive plague microorganisms in their bloodstreams. It reminded me of something. Typhus is one of the few diseases that a person can carry, yet still not be ill himself. Apparently the mutated form of typhus on this planet was very deadly. You either died—or were immune. People who came down with the disease were killed. So the present populace is descended from immune— and infected individuals. All of them."

"And our coming triggered it off," Pidik said.

"Unhappily true. There appears to be a relationship between this polyster allergy and their natural immunity. They first experience a massive allergic reaction. This breaks down their bodies' defenses and produces a synergistic reaction with the typhus, weakening their natural immunity. They get sick."

"But not anymore," Pidik said, firmly.

"No, not anymore. Now that we know the cause we know the cure. And the first one we are going to cure is Azpi-oyal, our ambassador of good will to his fellow Gudaegin. When he is cured he will believe in the cure. He will see the others treated and recovering. And if there are no more plague victims there is no further cause for war. We can deal with them, make peace, and get out of this tight corner we have maneuvered ourselves into.''

There was the sound of distant horns and massed shouting.

"I suggest you hurry," Dr. Bucuros said, turning to leave the room. "We are going to have a hard job of convincing them of anything if we are all dead."

In silent agreement they hurried after her.

➔ FROM FANATICISM, OR FOR REWARD

WONDERFUL! VERY CLEAR. The electronic sight was a new addition; he had used an ordinary telescopic sight when he test-fired the weapon, but it was no hindrance. The wide entrance to the structure across the street was sharp and clear despite the rain-filled night outside. His elbows rested comfortably on the packing crates that were placed before the slit he had cut through the outer wall of the building.

"There are five of them coming now. The one you want is the tallest." The radioplug in his ear whispered the words to him.

Across the street the men emerged. One was obviously taller than all the others. He was talking, smiling, and Jagen centered the scope on his white teeth, then spun the magnifier until teeth, mouth, tongue, filled the sight. Then a wide smile, teeth together, and Jagen squeezed his entire hand,

squeezed stock and trigger equally, and the gun
banged and jumped against his shoulder.

Now, quickly; there were five more cartridges
in the clip. Spin the magnifier back. He is falling.
Fire. He jerks. Fire. In the skull. Again. Fire.
Someone in the way: shoot through him. Fire. He
is gone. In the chest, the heart. Fire.

"All shots off," he said into the button before
his lips. "Five on target, one a possible."

"*Go,*" was all the radioplug whispered.

I'm going all right, he thought to himself; no
need to tell me that. The Greater Despot's police
are efficient.

The only light in the room was the dim orange
glow from the ready light on the transmatter. He
had personally punched out the receiver's code.
Three steps took him across the barren, dusty room,
and he slapped the actuator. Without slowing he
dived into the screen.

Bright glare hurt his eyes and he squinted against
it. An unshielded bulb above, rock walls, everything damp, a metal door coated with a patina of
rust. He was underground, somewhere, perhaps on
a planet across the galaxy, it didn't matter. There
was here. Everywhere was a step away with a
matter transmitter. Quickly, he moved to one side
of the screen.

Gas puffed out of it, expelled silently, then cut
off. Good. The other transmatter had been destroyed, blown up. Undoubtedly the police would
be able to trace his destination from the wreckage,
but it would take time. Time for him to obscure
his trail and vanish.

Other than the transmatter, the only object in the

stone cell was a large, covered ceramic vessel. He looked at the stock of his gun where he had pasted his instructions. Next to the number for this location was the notation *destroy gun*. Jagen peeled off the instructions and slipped them into his belt pouch. He took the lid from the vessel and turned away, coughing, as the fumes rose up. This bubbling, hellish brew would dissolve anything. With well-practiced motions he released the plastic stock from the weapon, then dropped it into the container. He had to step back as the liquid bubbled furiously and thicker fumes arose.

In his pouch was a battery operated saw, as big as his hand, with a serrated diamond blade. It buzzed when he switched it on, then whined shrilly when he pressed it against the barrel of the gun. He had measured carefully a few days earlier and had sawed a slight notch. Now he cut at that spot and in a few seconds half of the barrel clanged to the floor. It followed the stock into the dissolving bath, along with the clip that had held the bullets. His pouch yielded up another clip which he slipped into place in the gun. A quick jerk of his forefinger on the slide kicked the first cartridge into the chamber and he checked to be sure that the safety was on. Only then did he slip the truncated weapon up the loose sleeve of his jacket, so that the rough end of the sawn barrel rested against his hand.

It was shortened and inaccurate, but still a weapon, and still very deadly at short range.

Only when these precautions had been made did he consult the card and punch for his next destination. The instructions after this number read simply *change*. He stepped through.

Noise and sound, light and sharp smells. The ocean was close by, some ocean, he could hear the breakers and salt dampness was strong in his nose. This was a public communications plaza set around with transmatter screens, and someone was already stepping from the one he had used, treading on his heels. There were muttered words in a strange language as the man hurried away. The crowd was thick and the reddish sun, high above, was strong. Jagen resisted the temptation to use one of the nearby transmatters and walked quickly across the plaza. He stopped, then waited to follow the first person who passed him. This gave him a random direction that was not influenced by his own desires. A girl passed and he went after her. She wore an abbreviated skirt that ended just below her buttocks and had remarkably bowed legs. He followed their arcs down a side street. Only after they had passed one transmatter booth did he choose his own course. His trail was muddled enough now; the next transmatter would do.

There was the familiar green starburst ahead, above an imposing building, and his heart beat faster at the sight of the Greater Despot Police Headquarters. Then he smiled slightly; why not? The building was public and performed many functions. There was nothing to be afraid of.

Yet there was of course fear, and conquering it was a big part of the game. Up the steps and past the unseeing guards. A large rotunda with a desk in the middle, stands and services against the wall. And there, a row of transmatter screens. Walking at a steady pace he went to one of the center screens and punched the next code on his list.

The air was thin and cold, almost impossible to breathe, and his eyes watered at the sudden chill. He turned quickly to the screen to press the next number when he saw a man hurrying toward him.

"Do not leave," the man called out in intergalact.

He had a breath mask clipped over his nose and he held a second one out to Jagen, who quickly slipped it on. The warmed, richer air stayed his flight, as did the presence of the man who had obviously been expecting him. He saw now that he was on the bridge of a derelict spacer of ancient vintage. The controls had been torn out and the screens were blank. Moisture was condensing on the metal walls and forming pools upon the floor. The man saw his curious gaze.

"This ship is in orbit. It has been for centuries. An atmosphere and gravity plant were placed aboard while this transmatter is operating. When we leave an atomic explosion will destroy everything. If you are tracked this far the trail will end here."

"Then the rest of my instructions—?"

"Will not be needed. It was not certain this ship would be prepared in time, but it has been."

Jagen dropped the card, evidence, onto the floor, along with the radioplug. It would vanish with the rest. The man rapidly pressed out a number.

"If you will proceed," he said.

"I'll follow you."

The man nodded, threw his breath mask aside, then stepped through the screen.

They were in a normal enough hotel room, the kind that can be found on any one of ten thousand planets. Two men, completely dressed in black, sat in arm chairs watching Jagen through dark

glasses. The man who had brought him nodded
silently, pressed a combination on the transmatter,
and left.

"It is done?" one of the men asked. In addition
to the loose black clothing they wore black gloves
and hoods, with voice demodulators clamped across
their mouths. The voice was flat, emotionless,
impossible to identify.

"The payment," Jagen said, moving so that his
back was to the wall.

"We'll pay you, man, don't be foolish. Just tell
us how it came out. We have a lot invested in
this." The voice of the second man was just as
mechanically calm, but his fingers were clasping
and unclasping as he talked.

"The payment." Jagen tried to keep his voice
as toneless as their electronic ones.

"Here, hunter, now tell us," the first one said,
taking a box from the side table and throwing it
across the room. It burst open at Jagen's feet.

"All six shots were fired at the target I was
given," he said, looking down at the golden notes
spilling onto the floor. So much, it was as they
had promised. "I put four shots into the head, one
into the heart, one into a man who got in the way
that may have penetrated. It was as you said. The
protective screen was useless against mechanically
propelled plastic missiles."

"The paragrantic is ours," the second man intoned emotionlessly, but this was the machine in-
terpretation, for his excitement was demonstrated
by the manner in which he hammered on his chair
arm and drummed his feet.

Jagen bent to pick up the notes, apparently looking only at the floor.

The first man in black raised an energy pistol that had been concealed in his clothing and fired it at Jagen.

Jagen, who as a hunter always considered being hunted, rolled sideways and clutched the barrel of the shortened projectile weapon. With his other hand he found the trigger through the cloth of his sleeve and depressed it. The range was point-blank and a miss was impossible to a man of his experience.

The bullet caught the first man in the midriff and folded him over. He said *yahhhhh* in a very drab and monotonous way. The pistol dropped from his fingers and fell to the floor and he was obviously dead.

"Soft alloy bullets," Jagen said. "I saved a clip of them. Far better than those plastic things you supplied. Go in small, mushroom, come out big. I saved the gun, too, at least enough of it to still shoot. You were right; it should be destroyed to remove evidence, but not until after this session. And it doesn't show on an energy detector screen. So you thought I was unarmed. Your friend discovered the truth the hard way. How about you?" He talked quickly as he struggled to recover the gun that recoil had pulled from his hand and jammed into the cloth of his sleeve. There, he had it.

"Do not kill me," the remaining man said, his voice flat, though he cringed back and waved his hands before his face. "It was his idea, I wanted nothing to do with it. He was afraid that we could be traced if you were captured." He glanced at the folded figure, then quickly away as he became aware of the quantity of blood that was dripping from it. "I have no weapon. I mean you no harm. Do not kill me. I will give you more money." He was pleading for his life but the words came out as drab as a shopping list.

Jagen raised his weapon and the man writhed and cringed.

"Do you have the money with you?"

"Some. Not much. A few thousand. I'll get you more."

"I'm afraid that I cannot wait. Take out what you have—slowly—and throw it over here."

It was a goodly sum. The man must be very rich to carry this much casually. Jagen pointed the gun to kill him, but at the last instant changed his mind. It would accomplish nothing. And at the moment he was weary of killing. Instead he crossed over and tore the man's mask off. It was anti-climatic. He was fat, old, jowly—crying so hard that he could not see through his tears. In disgust Jagen hurled him to the floor and kicked him hard in the face. Then left. Ever wary he kept his body between the moaning man and the keys so there would be no slightest chance for him to see the number punched. He stepped into the screen.

The machine stepped out of the screen in the office of the Highest Officer of Police, many light years distant, at almost the same instant, on the planet where the assassination had taken place.

"You are Follower?" the officer asked.

"I am," the machine said.

It was a fine-looking machine, shaped in the form of a man. But that of a large man, well over two meters tall. It could have been any shape at all, but this form was a convenience when traveling among men. The roughly humanoid form was the only concession made. Other than having a torso, four limbs and a head, it was strictly functional. Its lines were smooth and flowing, and its metal shape coated with one of the new and highly resistant golden-tinted alloys. The ovoid that was its head was completely featureless, except for a T-shaped slit in the front. Presumably seeing and hearing devices were concealed behind the narrow opening, as well as a speech mechanism that parodied the full-timbered voice of a man.

"Do I understand, Follower, that you are the only one of your kind?" The police officer had become old, gray, and lined in the pursuit of his profession, but he had never lost his curiosity.

"Your security rating permits me to inform you that there are other Followers now going into operation, but I cannot reveal the exact number."

"Very wise. What is it that you hope to do?"

"I shall follow. I have detection apparatus far more delicate than any used in the field before. That is why my physical bulk is so great. I have the memory core of the largest library and means of adding to it constantly. I will follow the assassin."

"That may prove difficult. He—or she—destroyed the transmatter after the killing."

"I have ways of determining the tuning from the wreckage."

"The path will be obscured in many ways."

"None of them shall avail. I am the Follower."

"This was a dirty business. I wish you luck. If one can wish luck to a machine."

"Thank you for the courtesy. I do not have human emotions, though I can comprehend them. Your feelings are understood and a credit mark is being placed on your file even though you had not intended the remark to accomplish that. Now I would like to see all the records of the assassination, and then I will go to the place where the killer escaped."

Twenty years of easy living had not altered Jagen very much: the lines in the corners of his eyes and the touch of gray at his temples improved his sharp features rather than detracting from them. He no longer had to earn his living as a professional hunter, so could now hunt for his own pleasure, which he did very often. For many years he had stayed constantly on the move, obscuring his trail, changing his name and identity a dozen times. Then he had stumbled across this backward planet, completely by chance, and had decided to remain. The jungles were primitive and the hunting tremendous. He enjoyed himself all of the time. The money he had been paid, invested wisely, provided him with ample income for all of his needs and supported the one or two vices to which he was addicted.

He was contemplating one of them now. For more than a week he had remained in the jungle, and it had been a good shoot. Now, washed, refreshed, rested, he savored the thought of something different. There was a pleasure hall he knew, expensive, of course, but he could get there exactly what he needed. In a gold dressing gown, feet up and a drink in his hand, he sat back and looked through the transparent wall of his apartment at the sun setting behind the jungle. He had never had much of an eye for art, but it would have taken a blind man to ignore the explosion of greens below, purple and red above. The universe was a very fine place.

Then the alignment bell signaled quietly to show that another transmatter had been tuned to his. He swung about to see Follower step into the room.

"I have come for you, assassin," the machine said.

The glass fell from Jagen's fingers and rolled a wet trail across the inlaid wood of the floor. He was always armed, but caution suggested that the energy pistol in the pocket of his robe would have little effect on this solidly built machine.

"I have no idea what you are talking about," he said, rising. "I shall call the police about this matter."

He walked toward the communicator—then dived past it into the room beyond. Follower started after him, but stopped when he emerged an instant later. Jagen had a heavy calibre, recoilless rifle with explosive shells that he used to stop the multiton amphibians in the swamps. The weapon held ten of the almost cannon-sized shells, and he emptied the clip, point-blank, at the machine.

The room was a shambles, with walls floor and ceiling ripped by the explosive fragments. He had a minor wound in his neck, and another in his leg, neither of which he was aware of. The machine stood, unmoved by the barrage, the golden alloy completely unscratched.

"Sit," Follower ordered. "Your heart is laboring too hard and you may be in danger."

"Danger!" Jagen said, then laughed strangely and clamped his teeth hard onto his lip. The gun slipped from his fingers as he groped his way to an undamaged chair and fell into it. "Should I worry about the condition of my heart when you are here—Executioner?"

"I am Follower. I am not an executioner."

"You'll turn me over to them. But first, tell me how you found me. Or is that classified?"

"The details are. I simply used all of the most improved location techniques and transmatter records to follow you. I have a perfect memory and had many facts to work with. Also, being a machine, I do not suffer from impatience."

Since he was still alive, Jagen still considered escape. He could not damage the machine, but perhaps he could flee from it once again. He had to keep it talking.

"What are you going to do with me?"

"I wish to ask you some questions."

Jagen smiled inwardly, although his expression did not change. He knew perfectly well that the Greater Despot had more than this in mind for an assassin who had been tracked for twenty years.

"Ask them, by all means."

"Do you know the identity of the man you shot?"

"I'm not admitting I shot anyone."

"You admitted that when you attempted to assault me."

"All right. I'll play along." Keep the thing talking. Say anything, admit anything. The torturers would have it out of him in any case. "I never knew who he was. In fact I'm not exactly sure what world it was. It was a rainy place; I can tell you that much."

"Who employed you?"

"They didn't mention any names. A sum of money and a job of work were involved, that was all."

"I can believe that. I can also tell you that your heartbeat and pulse are approaching normal, so I may now safely inform you that you have a slight wound on your neck."

Jagen laughed and touched his finger to the trickle of blood.

"My thanks for the unexpected consideration. The wound is nothing."

"I would prefer to see it cleaned and bandaged. Do I have your permission to do that?"

"Whatever you wish. There is medical equipment in the other room." If the thing left the room he could reach the transmatter!

"I must examine the wound first."

Follower loomed over him—he had not realized the great bulk of the machine before—and touched a cool metal finger to the skin on his neck. As soon as it made contact he found himself completely paralyzed. His heart beat steadily, he breathed easily, his eyes stared straight ahead. But he could not move or speak, and could only scream wordlessly to himself in the silence of his brain.

"I have tricked you since it was necessary to have your body in a relaxed state before the operation. You will find the operation is completely painless.''

The machine moved out of his fixed point of vision and he heard it leave the room. Operation? What operation? What unmentionable revenge did the Greater Despot plan? How important was the man whom he had killed? Horror and fear filled his thoughts, but did not affect his body. Steadily, the breath flowed in and out of his lungs, while his heart thudded a stately measure. His consciousness was imprisoned in the smallest portion of his brain, impotent, hysterical.

Sound told him that the machine was now standing behind him. Then he swayed and was pushed from side to side. What was it doing? Something dark flew by a corner of his vision and hit the floor. What? WHAT!

Another something, this one spattering on the floor before him. Foamed, dark, mottled. It took long seconds for the meaning of what he saw to penetrate his terror.

It was a great gobbet of depilatory foam, speckled and filled with dissolved strands of his hair. The machine must have sprayed the entire can onto his head and was now removing all of his hair. But why? Panic ebbed slightly.

Follower came around and stood before him, then bent and wiped its metal hands on his robe.

"Your hair has been removed." *I know, I know! Why?* "This is a needed part of the operation and creates no permanent damage. Neither does the operation."

While it was speaking a change was taking place in Follower's torso. The golden alloy, so impervious to the explosives, was splitting down the center and rolling back. Jagen could only watch, horrified, unable to avert his gaze. There was a silvered concavity revealed in the openings, surrounded by devices of an unknown nature.

"There will be no pain," Follower said, reaching forward and seizing Jagen's head with both hands. With slow precision it pulled him forward into the opening until the top of his head was pressed against the metal hollow. Then, mercifully, unconsciousness descended.

Jagen did not feel the thin, sharpened needles that slid through holes in the metal bowl, then penetrated his skin, down through the bone of his skull and deep into his brain. But he was aware of the thoughts, clear and sharp, as if they were new experiences that filled his brain. Memories, brought up and examined, then discarded. His childhood, a smell, sounds he had long since forgotten, a room, grass underfoot, a young man looking at him, himself in a mirror.

This flood of memories continued for a long time, guided and controlled by the mechanism inside Follower. Everything was there that the machine needed to know and bit by bit it uncovered it all. When it was finished the needles withdrew into their sheaths and Jagen's head was freed. Once more he was seated upright in the chair—and the paralysis was removed as suddenly as it had begun. He clutched the chair with one hand and felt across the smooth surface of his skull with the other.

"What have you done to me? What was the operation?"

"I have searched your memory. I now know the identity of the people who ordered the assassination."

With these words the machine turned and started towards the transmatter. It had already punched out a code before Jagen called hoarsely after it.

"Stop! Where are you going? What are you going to do with me?"

Follower turned. "What do you want me to do with you? Do you have feelings of guilt that must be expunged?"

"Don't play with me, machine. I am human and you are just a metal thing. I order you to answer me. Are you from the Greater Despot's police?"

"Yes."

"Then you are arresting me?"

"No. I am leaving you here. The local police may arrest you, though I have been informed that they are not interested in your case. However I have appropriated all of your funds as partial payment for the cost of tracking you." It turned once more to leave.

"Stop!" Jagen sprang to his feet. "You have taken my money, I can believe that. But you cannot toy with me. You did not follow me for twenty years just to turn about and leave me. I am an assassin—remember?"

"I am well aware of the fact. That is why I have followed you. I am also now aware of your opinion of yourself. It is a wrong one. You are not unique or gifted or even interesting. Any man can kill when presented with the correct motivation. After all, you are animals. In time of war good young men drop bombs on people they do not know, by pressing switches, and this murder does not bother them in the slightest. Men kill to protect their families and are commended for it. You, a professional hunter of animals, killed another animal, who happened to be a man, when presented with enough payment. There is nothing noble, brave, or even interesting in that. That man is dead and killing you will not bring him to life. May I leave now?''

"No! If you do not want me—why spend those years following me? Not just for a few remnants of fact."

The machine stood straight, high, glowing with a mechanical dignity of its own, which perhaps reflected that of its builders.

"Yes. Facts. You are nothing, and the men who hired you are nothing. But why they did it and how they were able to do it is everything. One man, ten men, even a million are as nothing to the Greater Despot who numbers the planets in his realm in the hundreds of thousands. The Greater Despot deals only in societies. Now an examination will be made of your society and particularly of the society of the men who hired you. What led them to believe that violence can solve anything? What were the surroundings where killing was condoned or ignored—or accepted—that shaped their lives so that they exported this idea?

"It is the society that kills, not the individual.

"You are nothing," Follower added—could it have been with a touch of malice?—as it stepped into the screen and vanished.

➔ *HEAVY DUTY*

"BUT WHY YOU?" she asked.

"Because it happens to be my job." He clicked the last belt loop into place on his pack and shifted its weight comfortably on his shoulders.

"I don't understand why those men, the ones flying the delivery ship, why they couldn't have looked around first. To help you out a little bit, perhaps let you know what you were getting into. I don't think it's fair."

"It's very fair," he told her, tightening up one notch on the left shoulder strap and trying to keep his temper. He did not like her to come here when he was leaving, but there was no easy way to stop her. Once again he explained.

"The men who fly the contact ships have a difficult time of it just staying alive and sane, trapped in their ships while they go out to the stars. Theirs is a specialized job, only certain men with particular dispositions can survive the long flight. These same characteristics are outstandingly unsuited to planetary contact and exploration. It is work enough for them to do a high-level instrument and photographic sweep, and then to drop a transmatter screen on retrojets at a suitable spot. Bu the time the transmatter touches down and sends back their report they are well on their way to the next system. They've done their job. Now I'll do mine.''

"Ready for me yet, Specialist Langli?'' a man asked, looking in through the ready-room door.

"Just about,'' Langli said, disliking himself for the relief he felt at the other's intrusion. "Artificer Meer, this is my wife, Keriza.''

"A great honor, Wife Keriza. You must be proud of your husband.''

Meer was young and smiled when he talked, so it could be assumed that he was sincere about what he said. He wore a throat mike and earphones and was in constant contact with the computer.

"It is an honor,'' Keriza said, but could not prevent herself from adding, "but not an eternal one. This is a first betrothal and it expires in a few days, while my husband is away.''

"Fine,'' Artificer Meer said, not hearing the bitterness behind her words. "You can look forward to a second or final when he returns. A good excuse for a celebration. Shall I begin, Specialist?''

"Please do,'' Langli said, lifting his canteen with his fingertips to see if it was full.

Keriza retreated against the wall of the drab room while the checklist began; she was already left out. The computer murmured its questions into the artificer's ear and he spoke them aloud in the same machine-made tones. Both men attended to the computer, not to her, alike in their dark-green uniforms, almost the same color as the green-painted walls. The orange and silver of her costume was out of place here and she unconsciously stepped backward toward the entrance.

The checklist was run through quickly and met the computer's approval. Far more time was then taken up making the needed adjustments on Langli's manpower gear. This was a powered metal harness that supported his body, conforming to it like a flexible exoskeleton. It was jointed at his joints and could swivel and turn to follow any motion. Since the supporting pads were an integral part of his uniform, and the rods were thin and colored to match the cloth, it was not too obvious. An atomic energy supply in his pack would furnish power for at least a year.

"Why are you wearing that metal cage?" Keriza asked. "You have never done that before." She had to repeat her question, louder, before either man noticed her.

"It's for the gravity," her husband finally told her. "There's a two point one five three plus G on this planet. The manpower can't cancel that, but it can support me and keep me from tiring too quickly."

"You didn't tell me that about this planet. In fact you have told me nothing—"

"There's little enough. High gravity, cold and windy where I'm going. The air is good; it's been tested, but oxygen is a little high. I can use it."

"But animals, wild animals, are there any of them? Can it be dangerous?"

"We don't know yet, but it appears peaceable enough. "Don't worry about it." This was a lie, but one officially forced upon him. There were human settlers on this new planet, and this was classified information. A public announcement would be made only after official appraisal of his report.

"Ready," Langli said, pulling on his gloves. "I want to go before I start sweating inside this suit."

"Suit temperature is thermostatically controlled, Specialist Langli. You should not be uncomfortable."

He knew that: he just wanted to leave. Keriza should not have come here.

"Restricted country from here in," he told her, taking her arms and kissing her quickly. "I'll send you a letter as soon as I have time."

He loved her well enough, but not here, not when he was going on a mission. The heavy door closed behind them, shutting her out, and he felt relieved at once. Now he could concentrate on the job.

"Message from control," the artificer said when they entered the armored transmatter room through the thick triple doors. "They want some more vegetation and soil samples. Life forms and water, though these last can wait."

"Will comply," Langli said, and the artificer passed on the answer through his microphone.

"They wish you quick success, Specialist," the artificer said in his neutral voice, then, more warmly, "I do, too. It is a privilege to have

assisted you.'' He covered the microphone with
his hand. ''I'm studying, a specialist course, and
I've read your reports. I think that you . . . I mean
what you have done. . . .'' His words died and his
face reddened. This was a breach of rules and he
could be disciplined.

''I know what you mean, Artificer Meer, and I
wish you all the best of luck.'' Langli extended his
hand and, after a moment's reluctance, the other
man took it. Though he would not admit it aloud,
Langli was warmed by this irregular action. The
coldness of the transmatter chamber, with its gun
snouts and television cameras, had always depressed
him. Not that he wanted bands or flags when he
left, but a touch of human contact made up for a
lot.

''Goodby, then,'' he said, and turned and activated the switch on the preset transmatter control.
The wire lattice of the screen vanished and was
replaced by the watery blankness of the operating
Bhattacharya field. Without hesitating Langli stepped
into it.

An unseen force seized him, dragging him forward, hurling him face first to the ground. He
threw his arms out to break his fall and the safety
rods on his wrists shot out ahead of his hands,
telescoping slowly to soften the shock of impact; if
they had not he would surely have broken both his
wrists. Even with this aid the breath was knocked
from him by the impact of the manpower pads. He
gasped for air, resting on all fours. His mouth
burned with the coldness of it and his eyes watered. The uniform warmed as the icy atmosphere
hit the thermocouples. He looked up.

A man was watching him. A broad, solidly built man with an immense flowing black beard. He was dressed in red-marked leather and furs and carried a short stabbing spear no longer than his forearm. It was not until he moved that Langli realized he was standing up—not sitting down. He was so squat and wide that he appeared to be truncated.

First things came first: control had to have its samples. He kept a wary eye on the bearded man as he slipped a sample container from the dispenser on the side of his pack and put it flat on the ground. The ground was hard but ridged like dried mud, so he broke off a chunk and dropped it into the middle of the red plastic disc. Ten seconds later, as the chemicals in the disc reacted with the air, the disc curled up on the edges and wrapped the soil in a tight embrace. The other man shifted his spear from hand to hand and watched this process with widening eyes. Langli filled two more containers with soil, then three others with grass and leafy twigs from a bush a few feet away. This was enough. Then he backed slowly around the scarred bulk of the retrorockets until he stood next to the transmatter screen. It was operating but unfocused: anything entering it now would be broken down into Y-radiation and simply sprayed out into Bhattacharya space. Only when he pressed his hand to the plate on the frame would it be keyed to the receiver; it would operate for no one else. He touched the plate and threw the samples through. Now he could turn to the more important business.

"Peace," he said, facing the other man with his hands open and extended at his sides. "Peace."

The man did nothing in response, though he raised the spear when Langli took a step toward him. When Langli returned to his original position he dropped the spear again. Langli stood still and smiled.

"It's a waiting game, is it? You want to talk while we're waiting?" There was no answer, nor did he really expect one. "Right then, what is it we're waiting for? Your friends, I imagine. All of this shows organization, which is very hopeful. Your people have a settlement nearby, that's why the transmatter was dropped here. You investigated it, found no answers, then put a guard on it. You must have signaled them when I arrived, though I was flat on my face and didn't see it."

There was a shrill squealing behind a nearby slope that slowly grew louder. Langli looked on with interest as a knot of bearded men, at this distance looking very much like his guard, struggled into sight. They were all pulling a strange conveyance which had three pairs of wooden wheels: the apparently unoiled axles were making the squealing. It was no more than a padded platform on which rested a man dressed in bright-red leather. The upper part of his face was hidden by a metal casque pierced with eyeslits, but from below the rim a great white beard flowed across his chest. In his right hand the man held a long, thin-bladed carving knife which he pointed at Langli as he slowly stepped down from the conveyance. He said something incomprehensible in a sharp hoarse voice at the same time.

"I'm sorry, but I cannot understand you," Langli said.

At the sound of his words the old man started back and nearly dropped the weapon. At this sudden action the other men crouched and raised their spears toward Langli. The leader disapproved of this and shouted what could only have been commands. The spears were lowered at once. When he was satisfied with the reaction the man turned back to Langli and spoke slowly, choosing his words with care.

"I did not know . . . think . . . I would these words hear spoken by another. I know it only to read." The accent was strange but the meaning was perfectly clear.

"Wonderful. I will learn your language, but for now we can speak mine. . . ."

"Who are you? What is it . . . the thing there, it fell at night with a loud noise. How come you here?"

Langli spoke slowly and clearly, what was obviously a prepared speech.

"I come with greetings from my people. We travel great distances with this machine you see before you. We are not from this world. We will help you in many ways which I will tell you. We can help the sick and make them well. We can bring food if you are hungry. I am here alone and no more of us will come unless you permit it. In return for these things we ask only that you answer my questions. When the questions are answered we will answer any questions that you may have."

The old man stood with his legs widespread and braced, unconsciously whetting the blade on his leg. "What do you want here? What are your real needs . . . desires?"

"I have medicine and can help the sick. I can get food. I ask only that you answer my questions, nothing more."

Under the flowing moustache the old man's lips lifted in a cold grin. "I understand. Do as you say—or nothing will happen. Come with me, then." He stepped backward and settled slowly onto the cart which creaked with his weight. "I am Bekrnatus. You have a name?"

"Langli. I will be happy to accompany you."

They went in a slow procession over the crest of the rise and down into the shallow valley beyond. Langli was already tired, his heart and lungs working doubly hard to combat the increased gravity, and was exhausted before they had gone a quarter of a mile.

"Just a moment," he said. "Can we stop for a short while?"

Bekrnatus raised his hand and spoke a quick command. The procession stopped and the men immediately sat, most of them sprawling out horizontally in the heavy grass. Langli unclipped his canteen and drank deeply. Bekrnatus watched every move closely.

"Would you like some water?" Langli asked, extending the canteen.

"Very much," the old man said, taking the canteen and examining it closely before drinking from it. "The water has a taste of very difference. Of what metal is this . . . container made?"

"Aluminum I imagine, or one of its alloys."

Should he have answered that question? It certainly seemed harmless enough. But you never could tell. Probably he shouldn't have, but he was too tired to really care. The bearded men were watching intently and the nearest one stood up, staring at the canteen.

"Sorry," Langli said, blinking a redness of fatigue from his eyes and extending the canteen to the man. "Would you like a drink as well?"

Bekrnatus screamed something hoarsely as the man hesitated a moment—then reached out and clutched the canteen. Instead of drinking from it he turned and started to run away. He was not fast enough. Langli looked on, befuddled, as the old man rushed by him and buried his long knife to the hilt in the fleeing man's back.

None of the others moved as the man swayed, then dropped swiftly and heavily to the ground. He lay on his side, eyes open and blood gushing from his mouth, the canteen loose in his fingers. Bekrnatus kneeled and took away the canteen, then jerked the knife out with a single powerful motion. The staring dead eyes were still.

"Take this water thing and do not come . . . go near other people or give them anything."

"It was just water—"

"It was not the water. You killed this man."

Langli, befuddled, started to tell him that it was perfectly clear who had killed him, then wisely decided to keep his mouth shut. He knew nothing about this society and had made a mistake. That was obvious. In a sense the old man was right and he *had* killed the man. He fumbled out a stimulant tablet and washed it down with water from the offending canteen. The march resumed.

The settlement was in the valley, huddled against the base of a limestone cliff, and Langli was ex-

hausted when they reached it. Without the manpower he could not have gone a quarter of this
distance. He was in among the houses before he
realized they were there, so well did they blend
into the landscape. They were dugouts, nine-tenths
below the ground, covered with flat sod roofs; thin
spirals of smoke came from chimney openings in
most of them. The procession did not stop, but
threaded its way through the dug-in houses and
approached the cliff. This had a number of ground-
level openings cut into it, the larger ones sealed
with log doors. When they were closer Langli saw
that two windowlike openings were covered with
glass or some other transparent substance. He
wanted to investigate this—but it would have to
wait. Everything would have to wait until he regained a measure of strength. He stood, swaying,
while Bekrnatus climbed slowly down from the
wheeled litter and approached a log door which
opened as he came near. Langli started after him—
then found himself falling, unable to stand. He had
a brief moment of surprise, before the ground
came up and hit him, when he realized that for the
first time in his life he was fainting.

The air was warm on his face and he was lying
down. It took him some moments, even after he
had opened his eyes, to realize where he was. An
immense fatigue gripped him and every movement
was an effort; even his thoughts felt drugged. He
looked about the darkened room several times before the details made any meaning. A window that
was set deep into the stone wall. The dim bulk of
furniture and unknown objects. A weaker, yellow
light from the fire on the grate. A stone fireplace

and stone walls. Memory returned and he realized that he must be in one of the rooms he had noticed, hollowed out of the face of the cliff. The fire crackled; there was the not-unpleasant odor of pungent smoke in the air; soft, slapping footsteps came up behind him. He felt too tired to turn his head, but he banished this unworkmanlike thought and turned in that direction.

A girl's face, long blond hair, deep blue eyes.

"Hello. I don't believe we have met," he said.

The eyes widened, shocked, and the face vanished. Langli sighed wearily and closed his own eyes. This was a very trying mission. Perhaps he should take a stimulant. In his pack—

His pack! He was wide awake at the thought, struggling to sit up. They had taken his pack from him! At the same instant of fear he saw it lying next to the cot where it had been dropped. And the girl returned, pressing him back to a lying position. She was very strong.

"I'm Langli. What's your name?"

She was attractive enough, if you liked your girls squarefaced. Good bust, filled the soft leather dress nicely. But that was about all. Too broad-shouldered, too hippy, too much muscle. Very little different really from the other natives of this heavy planet. He realized that her eyes had never left his while he had been looking her up and down. He smiled.

"Langli is my name, but I suppose I shall never learn yours. The leader—what did he call himself—Bekrnatus, seems to be the only one who speaks a civilized tongue. I suppose I shall have to learn the local grunts and gurgles before I will be able to talk to you?''

"Not necessarily," she said, and burst out laughing at the surprised look on his face. Her teeth were even, white, and strong. "My name is Patna. Bekrnatus is my father.''

"Well, that's nice." He still felt dazed. "Sorry if I sounded rude. The gravity is a little strong for me.''

"What is gravity?''

"I'll tell you later, but I must talk to your father first. Is he here?''

"No. But he will be soon back. Today he killed a man. He must now the man's wife and family look after. They will go to another. Can I not answer your questions?''

"Perhaps." He touched the button on his waist that switched on the recorder. "How many of your people speak my language?''

"Just me. And Father, of course. Because we are The Family and the others are The People." She stood very straight when she said it.

"How many are there, of The People I mean?''

"Almost six hundred. It was a better winter than most. The air was warmer than in other years. Of course there was more—what is the word?— more rot in the stored food. But people lived.''

"Is winter over yet?''

She laughed. "Of course. It is almost the warmest time now.''

And they believe that this is warm, he thought. What can the winters be possibly like? He shivered at the thought.

"Please tell me more about The Family and The People. How are they different?"

"They just are, that is all," she said and stopped, as though she had never considered the question before. "We live here and they live there. They work and they do what we tell them to do. We have the metal and the fire and the books. That is how we talk your language, because we read what is written in the books."

"Could I see the books?"

"No!" She was shocked at the thought. "Only The Family can see them."

"Well—wouldn't you say that I qualify as a member of The Family? I can read, I carry many things made of metal." At that moment he realized what the trouble had been with his canteen. It was made of metal, for some reason taboo among most of these people. "And I can make fire." He took out his lighter and thumbed it so that a jet of flame licked out.

Patna looked at this, wide-eyed. "Our fires are harder to make. But, still, I am not sure. Father will know if you should look at the books." She saw his expression and groped around for some compromise. "But there is one book, a little book, that Father lets me have for my own. It is not an important book, though."

"Any book is important. May I see it?"

She rose hesitantly and went to the rear of the room, to a log door let into the stone, and tugged at the thick bars. When it was open she groped into the darkness of another room, a deeper cavern cut into the soft stone of the cliff. She returned quickly and resealed the door.

"Here," she said, holding it out to him, "you may read my book."

Langli struggled to a sitting position and took it from her. It was crudely bound in leather—the original cover must have worn out countless years earlier—and it crackled when he opened it. The pages were yellowed, frayed, and loose from the backbone. He poked through them, squinting at the archaic typeface in the dim light from the window, then turned back to the title page.

"Selected Poems," he read aloud. "Published at, I've never heard of the place, in . . . this is more important . . . 785 P.V. I think I've heard of that calendar, just a moment."

He put the book down carefully and bent to his pack, almost losing his balance as the more than doubled gravity pulled at him. His exoskeleton hummed and gave him support. The handbook was right on top and he flipped through it.

"Yes, here it is. Only went to 913 in their reckoning. Now to convert to Galactic Standard. . . ." He did some silent figuring and put the handbook away, taking up the other book again. "Do you like poetry?" he asked.

"More than anything. Though I only have these. There are no other poems in the books. Though of course there are *some* others. . . ."

She lowered her eyes and, after a moment's thought, Langli realized why.

"These others, you wrote them yourself, didn't you? You must tell me one sometime—"

There was a sudden rattling at the bolts that sealed the front door and Patna tore the book from his hands and ran with it to the dark end of the room.

Bekrnatus pushed open the door and came in wearily. "Close it," he ordered as he threw aside his helmet and dropped into a padded lounge, half bed, half chair. Patna moved quickly to do his bidding.

"I am tired, Langli," he said, "and I must sleep. So tell me what you are doing here, what this all means."

"Of course. But a question or two first. There are things I must know. What do your people do here, other than sleep and eat and gather food?"

"The question makes no sense."

"I mean anything. Do they mine and smelt metal? Do they carve, make things from clay, paint pictures, wear jewelry—"

"Enough. I understand your meaning. I have read of these things, seen pictures of them. Very nice. In answer to your question—we do nothing. I could never understand how these things were done and perhaps you will tell me when it suits you to answer questions rather than ask them. We live, that is hard enough. When we have planted our food and picked our food we are through. This is a hard world and the act of living takes all of our time."

He barked a harsh command in the local language, and his daughter shuffled to the fireplace. She returned with a crude clay bowl which she handed to him. He raised it to his lips and drank deeply, making smacking noises with his lips.

"Would you care for some?" he asked. "It is a drink we make; I do not know if there is a word for it in the book language. Our women chew roots and spit them into a bowl.''

"No, none thank you." Langli fought to keep his voice even, to control his disgust. "Just one last question. What do you know of your people coming to this world? You do know that you came here?''

"Yes, that I know, though little more. The story is told, though nothing is written, that we came from another world to this world, from the sky, though how it was done I know not. But it was done, for the books are not of this world and they have pictures of scenes not of this world. And there is the metal, and the windows. Yes, we came here.''

"Have others come? Like myself. Are there records?''

"None! That would have been written. Now you tell me, stranger from the metal box. What do you do here?''

Langli lay down, carefully, before he spoke. He saw that Patna was sitting as well. The gravity must be fought, constantly, unceasingly.

"First you must understand that I came from inside the metal box, then again I didn't. At night you see the stars and they are suns like the one that shines here, yet very distant. They have worlds near them, like this world here. Do you know what I am talking about?''

"Of course. I am not of The People. I have read of astronomy in the books.''

"Good. Then you should know that the metal box contains a transmatter which you must think of as a kind of door. One door that is at the same time two doors. I stepped through a door on my planet, very far away, and stepped out of your door here. All in an eyeblink of time. Do you understand?''

"Perhaps." Bekrnatus dabbed at his lips with the back of his hand. "Can you return the same way? Step into the box and come out on a planet, up there in the sky."

"Yes, I can do that."

"Is that how we came to this world?"

"No. You came by a ship of space, a large metal box built to move between the stars, in the years before the transmatter could be used at stellar distances. I know this because your window there is the window from a spacer, and I imagine your metal was salvaged from the ship as well. And I also know how long you have been here, since there was a date in the front of that poetry book your daughter showed me."

Patna gasped, a sharp intake of air, and Bekrnatus pulled himself to a sitting position. The clay bowl fell, unheeded, and shattered on the floor.

"You showed him a *book*," Bekrnatus hissed, and struggled to his feet.

"No, wait!" Langli said, realizing he had precipitated another crisis through ignorance. Would the man try to kill his daughter? He tore at his pack. "It was my fault, I asked for the book. But I have many books; here I'll show you. I'll give you some books. This . . . and this."

Bekrnatus did not heed the words, if he even heard them, but he stopped as the books were pushed before him. He reached for them hesitantly.

"Books," he said, dazedly. "Books, new books,

books I have never seen before. It is beyond wonder."

He clutched the books to his chest and half fell back into his chair. A good investment, Langli thought. Never was a first reader and a basic dictionary more highly prized.

"You can have all the books you want now. You can discover your history, all of it. I can tell you that your people have been here, roughly, about three thousand years. Your coming here may have been an accident; two things lead me to believe that. This is a very grim world with little to offer. I can't picture it being selected for colonization. Then there is the complete break with technology and culture. You have a few books, they could have been salvaged. And metal, perhaps from the wreck of the ship. That you have survived is little short of miraculous. You have this social or class distinction that has also passed down. Your ancestors were perhaps scientists, ship's officers, something that set them apart from ordinary men. And you have kept the distinction."

"I am tired," Bekrnatus said, turning the books over and over in his hands, "and there are many new things to think about all at once. We will talk tomorrow."

He dropped back, eyes closed, books still in his grasp. Langli was ready to sleep himself, exhausted by the efforts he had forced himself to. The light seemed to be fading; he wondered how long the local day was, and did not really care. He took an eight-hour sleeping pill from his medical kit and washed it down with water from his canteen. A night's sleep would make things look a good deal different.

During the night he was aware of someone moving about, going to the fire. At one time he thought he felt the soft touch of hair across his face and lips upon his forehead. But he could not be sure and thought it was probably a dream.

It was bright morning when he awoke, with the sun striking directly through the window, the shaft of light adding unexpected color to the gray stone of the back wall. Bekrnatus' couch was empty and Patna was working at the fireplace, humming quietly to herself. When he shifted position his bed squeaked and she turned to look at him.

"You are awake. I hope that you slept well. My father has gone out with the ax so wood can be chopped."

"You mean that he chops the wood?" Langli yawned, his head still thick with sleep.

"No, never. But the ax head is metal so he carries it and must be there when it is used. Your morning food is ready." She ladled one of the clay bowls full of gruel and brought it to him. He smiled and shook his head no.

"Thank you, that is very hospitable. But I cannot eat any of your food until laboratory analysis has been made—"

"You think I am trying to poison you?"

"Not at all. But you must realize that major metabolic changes take place in human beings cut off from the main stream. There may be chemicals in the soil here, in the plants, that you can ingest but that would be sure death for me. It smells wonderful, but it could hurt me. You wouldn't want that to happen?''

"No! Of course not." She almost hurled the bowl from her. "What will you eat?"

"I have my own food here, see."

He opened his pack and took out a mealcel, pulling the tab so the heating began. He was hungry, he realized, hungrier than he had ever felt before, and began spooning down the concentrate before the heat cycle was finished. His body needed nourishment, fighting constantly against the drag of gravity.

"Do you know what this is?" Patna asked, and he looked up to see her holding a brownish, ragged-edged fragment of some kind.

"No, I don't. It looks like wood or bark."

"It is the inner bark of a tree, we use it to write on, but that is not what I meant. I meant there is something *on* it. That is what I meant. . . ."

Even in the dim light Langli could realize that she was blushing. Poor girl, a literate among savages, trapped on this dismal and isolated world.

"I might guess," he said carefully. "Could it be one of the poems you wrote? If it is—I would like to hear it."

She shielded her eyes with her hand and turned away for a moment, a caricature of a shy maiden in a squat wrestler's body. Then she struggled with herself and started the poem in a weak voice, but continued, louder and louder.

> I dare not ask a kiss,
> I dare not beg a smile,
> Lest having that, or this,

I might grow proud the while.
No, no, the utmost share
Of my desire shall be
Only to kiss the air
That lately did kiss thee.

She almost cried the last words aloud, then
turned and fled to the far side of the room and
stood with her face against the wall. Langli groped
for the right words. The poem was good, whether
she had written it herself or copied it he did not
know—nor did it matter. It said what she wanted
to say.

"That's beautiful," he told her. "A really beautiful poem—"

Before he could finish she ran, feet slapping
hard against the floor, across the room and knelt
beside his bed. Her solid, powerful arms were
about him and her face against his, buried in the
pillow. He could feel the tear-wetness of her cheeks
against his own and her muffled voice in his ear.

"I knew you would come, I know who you are,
because you had to come from far away like a
knight in the poems riding a horse to save me.
You knew I needed you. My father, I, the only
Family left, I must marry one of The People. It
has been done before. Ugly, stupid, I hate them,
the brightest, we tried to teach him to read, he
couldn't, stupid. But you came in time. You are
The Family, you will take me. . . ."

The words died away and her lips found his,
urgent and strong with desire, and when he held
her shoulders and tried to push her away his exoskeleton whined with the effort but she did not

move. Finally, exhausted, she released him and pushed her face deep into the pillow again. He stood, swaying, bracing himself on the back of a chair. When he spoke it was with sincerity as he tried to make the truth less harsh than it really was.

"Patna, listen, you must believe me. I like you, you're a wonderful, brave girl. But this just can't be. Not because I am already married, that marriage will be terminated before I return, but because of this world. You can't leave it, and I would die if I stayed here. The adaptations your people have been forced to make to survive must be incredible. Your circulatory system alone must be completely different—your blood pressure much more than normal to get blood to your brain, with more muscles in the walls of the arteries to help pump it. Perhaps major valve changes and distribution. You can't possibly have children with anyone from off this planet. Your children would be stillborn, or die soon after birth, unfit. That is the truth, you must believe—"

"Ugly, skinny, too tall, too weak, shut up!" she screeched and lashed out at him, her head still turned away.

He tried to move aside, he could not, not fast enough. Her hand slapped against his arm with a sudden explosion of pain. A sharp cracking sound.

The bitch has broken my arm, he screamed to himself, staggering, sitting down slowly. His forearm hung crookedly in the brace of the exoskeleton and how it hurt. He cradled it on his knees and fumbled through his medical supplies with his good hand. She tried to help him and he snarled at her and she went away.

Bekrnatus came in, an ax over his shoulder, while the emergency cast was hardening and Langli was giving himself a shot of painkiller, with a tranquilizer for his nerves.

"What is wrong with your arm?" Bekrnatus asked, dropping the ax and falling into his couch.

"I had an accident. I will have to go get medical help from my people soon so I must talk to you now. Tell you what you need to know—"

"Do that. I have questions—"

"There is no time for questions." The pain was still there and he snapped the words out. "If I had the time I would explain everything slowly and in great detail so you would understand and agree. Now I will just tell you. If you want help you must pay for it. It costs a great deal to plant an MT screen on a planet as distant as this one. Medical supplies, food, energy sources, anything that we supply you will also cost a good deal. You will have to repay us."

"You have our thanks, of course."

"Not negotiable!" The pain was almost gone but he could feel the broken ends of the bones grate together when he moved. His nerves felt the same way despite the tranquilizer.

"Listen carefully and try to remember what I say. There is no pie in the sky. What you get for nothing is worth it. Out there are more planets than you could possibly count—and more people on them than *I* could count. And the transmatter makes them all next door neighbors. Can you imagine what hell that has wreaked with culture, government, finances, down through the millennia? No, I can see by your face that you can't. Then just think about this one bit of it. To further certain ends individuals form a cooperation, a sort of cross between a cooperative and a corporation, if those words are in any of your books. I belong to one of these called World Openers. We explore unsettled planets and occasionally contact worlds like yours that aren't on the MT net. For services rendered we demand payment in full.''

Patna had come to stand by her father, silently, her arm about his thick knobbed shoulders. Her face, as she looked at Langli, was a study in hatred, contempt. Bekrnatus, a lord on his own world, would still not comprehend the realities of the galaxy outside.

"We will pay what you ask, gladly, but pay with what? We have no money, none of the resources you were asking about last night."

"You have yourselves," Langli said, emotionlessly, as the drugs took hold. "Because that is all you have it will take generations to repay your debt. You will breed faster and better, and we will help you with that. For a price, of course. We have operations on heavy gravity worlds that must be supervised. Automatic machinery can't do everything. And there are others who can use workers of your type as well—"

"You come to enslave us, imprison us!" Bekrnatus roared. "To make free men into beasts of burden. Never!"

He grabbed up the ax from the floor and climbed to his feet, swinging it high. Langli was ready. His gun snapped just once and the explosion shook the room as a great pit was blown from the stone wall behind Bekrnatus.

"Just imagine what that would have done to you. Now sit down and don't be foolish. I will kill you to save my own life, be sure of that. We can't imprison you—because you are in prison already on this high-G world. The force that pulls you down, that makes things fall when dropped. This force is weaker on other worlds. I can leave and seal the transmatter and that will be the end of it. If that is what you really wish. The choice is yours to make." He waved the gun at Patna. "Now open that door."

Bekrnatus stood, the ax dangling forgotten from his hand; the world he knew had changed, everything changed. Langli struggled his pack to one shoulder and waved Patna aside. He moved slowly toward the door.

"I will return and you can tell me your decision then."

Patna called to him as he went out, fighting down her loathing.

"The transmatter, when will we get to use it? To see the wonders of other worlds—"

"Never in your lifetime. Use of the MT is granted only when all the debts are paid." He had to say it because the sooner she faced the truth the better she would adjust. "And you will be occupied elsewise. Intelligent operators will be needed, not strong backs. Yours is the only womb from which intelligence may spring on this world. Keep it busy."

He hobbled away until he was clear of the buildings, then gratefully set the pack down. It was too much of a burden to take back to the transmatter. He triggered the destruct and went on while it burned fiercely behind him. Expensive equipment, but it would go on the bill. They would choose to accept and pay; they really did not have much of a choice. It would be for their benefit. Not so much now, but in the long run. The two squat figures were still in the doorway looking after him and he turned quickly away.

What did they expect, charity? The universe was uncharitable. You had to pay for what you took from it. That was a natural law that could not be broken.

And he was doing his job, that was all.

It was just a job.

He was helping them.

Wasn't he?

Stumbling, sweating, and gasping, he hurried to be away from this place.

➔ A TALE OF THE ENDING

+No MORE could the Elstaran intermovement be stemmed when IJsselDijk a leader of men funneled sametyped through oneone and fortuned intramovement canceling all tendencies and Elstaran futures subsumed. End of sentence. End of paragraph. End of chapter. End of book. Type +

Dehan stretched widely as the screen before him darkened and, an instant later, his dictation appeared on it in a solid bank of type. He touched the screen in a few places with a stylus and made corrections, then nodded with satisfaction.

+Print+ he said and pushed away from his worktable. He saw that it was nearing seventy-five on the clock, almost the time he usually went swimming with Sousbois, but he was too tired for that now; the work had been intense and concentrated and he had labored at it steadily without getting enough sleep. He stretched again, yawning

as well this time, and went to lie gratefully on the
bed.

+ Lights off + he said and closed his eyes to the
velvety darkness and was asleep.

Eighty-four the clock read when he awoke and
he knew that Sousbois was long gone, but he still
wanted to bathe himself. Quickly stripping off his
daily clothes he put on a robe and went to the
right-hand Door, the one that, by habit, he always
used when going out. As he thought of the sunlight and the water his fingers automatically tapped
out the correct twelve-digit code on the signal
plate. The surface of the Door shimmered and he
stepped through.

From the cool underground room buried somewhere inside the solid stone of some planet he
walked out into the burning blue sunshine of the
Ytong shore. Gasping in lungfuls of the furnacelike
air he trotted quickly across the gold sand to the
water's edge where little waves rolled up, breaking
into hissing bubbles one after the other. Quickly,
for he could feel the sweat already dotting his
skin, he dropped his robe and kicked off his san-
dals and fell into the water. It closed a cool embrace about him and he sank, rose, wallowed
happily.

With just his head above the water he could see
the narrow strand vanishing off into the distance
on either hand. The gray wall of the escarpment
rose above it. As always when he looked at that
immense barrier of stone he wondered idly what
lay beyond it, although this was only a fleeting
interest. Someone here had told him that there was
probably only more stone since the land, like the

sea, sported no life forms at all. Below the cliff
and close to it were a number of Doors since this
was a popular bathing area. People hurried in and
out of them and the shallow water was dotted with
swimmers for as far as he could see in both directions. The water was very soothing, fresh and
transparent, and he ducked under to cool his head
and swam slowly along the featureless bottom.
When he surfaced he saw that a man had emerged
from the Door he had used and was trotting quickly
across the searing beach just as he had done. In a
moment the stranger was splashing heavily in the
shallows, submerging then surfacing nearby.

+ Linkica + the newcomer said when he saw
that he was not alone.

+ Dehan +

They paddled near each other for a few moments, observing the customary period of silence
in case either of them did not wish to converse at
this time. They remained close by.

+ The sun appears to have moved down toward
the water + Dehan said, squinting up at it.

+ Yes. It won't be long before we must find
another beach until it returns. I worked the figures
out from observations once. This planet has a
period of rotation of six thousand, four hundred
thirty time units. The day is three thousand, two
hundred fifteen long. Although it is too cold to
swim in the early morning +

+ You are a man of science? +

Dehan knew that the other must be of some high
standing or he would not have used this Door. The
ocean of Ytong was here to be enjoyed by anyone,
but Doornumbers were exchanged only among peo-

ple of the same levels of attainment. Somewhere on this beach was a child's Door. Perhaps a madman's Door; he neither knew nor cared.

+ I am a phylogeneticist +

Dehan nodded unknowingly and splashed water onto his head. Another long word. Another speciality. There must be thousands, perhaps millions of them. + I am a historicollator +

+ How interesting. I have always wanted to meet one +

Dehan closed both his eyes in the expression that meant humorous disbelief. + Can it be true? I have never met anyone other than another historicollator whoever heard of the speciality +

The other man rubbed his hairless scalp, now reddening under the sun, and smiled.

+ I can pretend no great breadth of knowledge. I must admit that I searched the word out as a reference. In relation to my own work of course . . . +

At the mention of his work he suffered a natural embarrassment and Dehan sank beneath the water and swam in a circle to lessen it. There are certain things that are never discussed while bathing. + I should like to close my pores + he said upon surfacing again. + And you? +

+ A fine suggestion + They waded ashore and quickly put on their robes.

+ I have recently visited a frigidarium that is very unusual + Linkica said hopefully, volunteering the information to excise the memory of his recent breach of conduct. He spoke the code number aloud, his fingers unconsciously tapping out the combinations of numerals in the air.

+ I do not know it. I will be pleased to follow you +

Happier now Linkica moved quickly to the Door and activated it. Dehan stepped through behind him and his body recoiled as the subzero air and swirling snow struck at him, gasping at the sudden shock. They appeared to be on an icy ridge that fell away into snow-clouded nothingness on both sides. Ahead, barely visible through the pelting flakes, were two other Doors set into the cliff face. Linkica had to shout into Dehan's ear to be heard.

+ When it is not snowing one can see impossibly far in this direction. Mountains, valleys, snow-cap, terribly impressive +

+ I shall . . . remember + Dehan stammered through numb lips.

They shuffled across the slippery ice surface, following the groove worn by other footsteps, sharply aware that only a single waist-high bar on either side stood between them and plummeting destruction. Gratefully they passed through the Door and into a robing room and each took a cubicle. Dehan sent his soiled robe through a small Door back to his own quarters, then dried and put on a one-use lounge suit from the dispenser. His skin tingled and he felt wonderful. That was certainly a fine frigidarium. He would try it again, hopefully on a clear day.

Linkica was waiting for him at a table by the immense window. The light of twin moons flooded the valley outside, filling it with infinite shades of gray and black where hills, jungle, and river met and merged. Dehan knew this place, built into a high hillside of some tropical world. They nodded, ordered drinks, then sipped at them when they appeared on the table.

+ What is your work? + Dehan asked. + Phylo-gen-something you said +

+ Phylogeneticist. I attempt to trace the origin of different species, ancestorship, relationships. Most useful in stockbreeding, food plants, that sort of thing +

Dehan nodded although he had no idea of what the man was talking about. Encouraged, Linkica went on.

+ Some time ago I was consulted about a gene-linked human disease. I traced its origin and found the correction that must be made. Because of this I became most interested in mankind, this most un-usual of all animals, and I began to trace our history. In some ways, one might say, there is a slight resemblance between my small labors and your great work. Are you working well of late? +

Dehan nodded and smiled. The man was good-mannered after all. One never discussed one's own work in detail until all present had mentioned theirs.

+ I have done with the Elstaran. A tedious task, a portion of history that was singularly dull as human history goes, and entirely too long for its own worth. A dozen suns, twenty or so planets, now thankfully gone by courtesy of a fortuitous supernova. I reduced over nine hundred volumes to a single volume, losing nothing of value in so doing +

+ Admirable. How we do need your sort of talent to pare the long ribbon of history to manage-able units. We would drown in the superfluous were it not for you. I can state this truthfully, for in my own research I have realized for the first time the incredible length of the history of our species. Would you say millions of time units? +

+ More. More + Dehan spoke the words slowly, with deep feeling.

+ That it could be so. I do believe it + Linkica bowed his head beneath the weight of the thought. + A moment for beauty, if you will. Sunrise is near and the sky changes +

They watched silently for a brief time. The sky was lightening with a tropical swiftness. Mist rose from the trees and river and the first muted pink brought color to the grays, touching the swirls and pools with an invisible brush. It was entrancing and they opened themselves to appreciate it.

+ I have uncovered strange curious quaint and mystifying facts along this endless trail of progress + Linkica said. + Have you ever considered why we count from a twelve-digit base? +

+ Mathematically it is the best. There are but eleven digits and the zero to remember. Yet still capable of infinite amplitude. Divisible as well by one, two, three, four, and six. A fine base +

+ That is all? +

+ That is enough +

+ Have you never considered that at some time, in the dawn of our race, we must have first started to count and in our simplicity used our fingers as a basic system + He spread his hands on the table and looked at his dozen fingers. + Could that not be possible? +

+ Possible. But just a theory. You might just as well say that if we had had five fingers on each hand we would have used ten as a base +

Linkica's face went white in an instant and he lifted his glass and drained it quickly. Control returned.

+An interesting number. Did you pick it by chance? Or has there been a system of mathematics using base ten in the same manner that computers use base two?+

+I do not remember. But we can find out easily enough+

Dehan strolled across the room to the computer outlet that graced all public places. He was experienced, greatly experienced, at ruthlessly tracking down the most stubbornly hidden facts, and this was simplicity itself in comparison. At all times he knew the right questions to ask. His fingers moved on the control squares constantly, changing the displays at almost the very instant they appeared. Through the local computer to the infinite computer, linked through transmatter connections to all the memory units in the galaxy, to mathematics and history and ever deeper. He returned quickly to the table and sipped his drink.

+An interesting fact discovered. At one time, oh dear, dear, how long ago, the base of ten was universally used. It was replaced by twelve, undoubtedly because of its superiority. So it appears that the finger theory must be dismissed+

+Not at once. My researches have disclosed that at one time a large proportion of mankind had but ten fingers+

+A coincidence+ Dehan did not believe the words even as he spoke them.

+Possibly. But if there is an explanation—what is it? If the two facts are interconnected the resulting logical equation can be read in one of two ways. When the shift from base ten to base twelve occurred there was a resulting change in the number of fingers +

+ Highly improbable +

+ I agree. Therefore we must consider the alternative that some great mutation, change, or conflict swept the human race. Perhaps there were opposing groups and the twelves won over the tens in a great war . . . +

+ There has never been a war like that. I would know +

+ Of course. But it is an interesting problem +

They sat in silence for a while, sipping their drinks and watching daylight come to the valley below them. The morning fog burned away as the first rays of the great orange sun struck through the mountain crags. There were crude dwellings beside the river and Dehan touched the window controls. Instantly the image expanded, so enlarged they appeared to be right in among the huts. A blue-skinned aborigine waddled through the doorway, yawning long saurian jaws to show impressive rows of pointed teeth. It picked up a stick and dug at some irritation in the deep folds of skin while looking on coldly at the growing activity around.

+ Time bound + Linkica said. + We were once that way, too. The ontological evidence is clear +

+ I do not know what you are referring to +

+ These creatures. Their life cycles are bound to the planetary rotation. They sleep during periods of darkness and are awake during their day +

+ How unnatural +

+Not at all. It is the natural outcome of a planetary existence. It has taken us thousands of generations to outgrow our dependence upon a waking-sleeping cycle, to reach the present point where we sleep for short periods whenever we feel tired+

+I can imagine no other way to sleep. And if this change were made, what possible reason could there be for it?+

+That appears obvious. The Doors. Their introduction must have altered every facet of existence+

Dehan raised his eyebrows. +Then you are not one of those who believe that the Doors have been with us from the dawn of time?+

+A child's myth. The Doors are artifacts that we still build. Though now they are single unit, solid block, solid-state construction, almost indestructible, they were not always that way. Earlier forms can be found in museums. Have you never wondered why there are always two Doors together, always?+

+I never considered. It is just the natural way of things+

+There is a reason. An engineer told me. Perfect as the Door mechanism is there can be, once in a very long while, a failure of mechanism. If this happens the other Door is always standing ready. There are many places where it would be embarrassing to be without a Door+

+Indeed!+ Dehan said and felt cold at the thought, thinking about his room. It was embedded in the solid rock of a world whose name he forgot. He had never been on its surface because it was airless. At one time it had been mined for precious metal, and great tunnels were driven through the heart of the stone mountains. When the ore was gone the tunnels had been plugged with molten slag. At intervals. Doors had been left in the boxlike openings to be furnished as private quarters. Very private. Without the Doors they were but bubbles in the rock. It would be a lonely, forgotten death for anyone trapped in one of them.

+Logic forces us to a single conclusion+ Linkica said. +There must have been a time, unimaginable as it is to us, when mankind did not possess the Doors+

+It follows then, that you are a monolinearist, not a multifontist?+

+Of course. For one thing it is biologically impossible to have a single species occur in a number of different places and then be able to interbreed. Just as there was a time when we had no Doors, so was there a time when we were confined to one restricted area of space+

+To but a single planet?+

Linkica smiled. +You said it—I did not. It carries the theory almost too far+

+Why? I do not tempt you into rash statements for I am as enthusiastic a monolinearist as you are, even though it is an unfashionable attitude to hold these days. I will go even further. I believe we did originate on a single planet at one time. Just as those creatures out there are natives of this world and incapable of leaving+

+You force agreement from me. I admit to physical change, but never considered that cultural change must accompany it. We may have originated from as crude a background as this one. If so—it had to be a single planet +

+ I have long thought so, and during my work have traced mankind's movements backward as far as possible. Always I have found the simpler growing into the complex. My researches have been exhaustive +

Linkica shielded his eyes for a moment in the sign of great appreciation. + Can it be that you have discovered this proto world, this home world? +

+ Perhaps. Though I doubt it. I have traced back all records, the oldest records, to an incredibly ancient world. I do not know if it is *the* planet, only that there are none older +

+ I humbly request the code +

+ A pleasure to share it + Dehan spoke the digits aloud. + In fact we could go there now and see it +

+ You are kinder than I thought possible +

+ I am pleased to take you. So few show any interest at all +

Dehan led the way through the Door to a small and crudely furnished room.

+ So rarely do people come here that it is sealed for the most part. See my visits on the graph. The first in many thousand units + He examined the controls and nodded with satisfaction. + Air, temperature, all is well +

They passed through a sealing door into a long, corridorlike room. There were viewing ports set into one wall while everywhere else were cabinets and displays.

+ Dead now + Linkica said, looking out on the

desiccated landscape. A sun, scarcely brighter than the other stars, shown as a cold, unblinking disc in the black sky. Air gone, water gone, life gone, bare sand and rock stretched flatly to the horizon. Yet nearby great monoliths, fissured and eroded, still bore witness of having been shaped by some intelligence.

+ These cases contain the few identifiable objects found here +

Linkica turned with a high anticipation that slowly faded and died.

+ These could be—anything + he said, pointing to the eroded lumps of metal and stone.

+ I know. But should we expect more? +

+ Of course not. You are correct +

Linkica looked once more at the mute age-old shapes, then out again at the dead plain. He shivered, although the room was warm and comfortable. + I feel the weight of ages here. More time than I can possibly understand has passed for this world. I see how short my own individual span of existence is and how unimportant +

+ I have felt the same thing myself, here, many times. It is said that a man's mind cannot encompass the idea of its own death, but when I am here I can begin to see how a species might die. If we had not had the Door we would be here, trapped here, dead here, if this were the only world we had ever known +

+ Give thanks it was not. Mankind is universal. We rule everywhere +

+ But for how long? Is not one galaxy—in the fullness of time—like one planet? Will it not die? Or could we not be displaced by some other creature? Something stronger, newer, better. I must admit that this is a recurrent nightmare I have. The Doors are everywhere. Might *one* of them not be in the wrong spot? A planet say where this other specie waits. To subtly move among us, displace us and end our existence for all time? +

+ It is possible + Linkica agreed. + All things are possible in the fullness of eternity. But it would be a painless conquest. We would never know. Why do you point? What is it? +

+ There. I wished to talk with you first before you saw this last artifact +

The lights grew brighter as they approached and the figure could be plainly seen. Painting or photograph, it lay beneath a thick, transparent coating and many details were visible despite its age.

+ What is this creature? + Linkica asked. + Very like a man, indeed. But look, it has fur upon its skull as we do not, nor does it have a nictitating membrane in its eyes. The anatomy is wrong, the joints—and look. Five fingers on each hand, ten in all— +

He stopped, struck silent by memory, and turned wide-eyed and numb toward Dehan who nodded slowly.

+ This is what frightens me. The word inscribed beneath the figure is the name of a leader so great that I have found references to him in a few sources. *Our* sources. Ancient records. It appears then, looking at this man . . . +

+ But *we* are men! +

+ Are we? We call ourselves men and have mankind's cultural heritage. But is it not possible that—as we theorized earlier—that mankind could be replaced? That we have indeed replaced them? +

+ Then—who are we? + A shudder passed through him at the thought.

+ We? We are mankind now. By cultural inheritance if not by blood line. But this is not what disturbs me. It is a more selfish thought +

For a long moment there was only silence in the lifeless room on a dead world.

+ I think always. What thing is waiting out there, that will sometime—perhaps even now—replace us? +

HARRY HARRISON

☐	48505-0	A Transatlantic Tunnel, Hurrah!	$2.50
☐	48540-9	The Jupiter Plague	$2.95
☐	48565-4	Planet of the Damned	$2.95
☐	48557-3	Planet of No Return	$2.75
☐	48031-8	The QE2 Is Missing	$2.95
☐	48554-9	A Rebel in Time	$3.50

POUL ANDERSON
Winner of 7 Hugos and 3 Nebulas

☐	53088-8	CONFLICT	$2.95
	53089-6		Canada $3.50
☐	48527-1	COLD VICTORY	$2.75
☐	48517-4	EXPLORATIONS	$2.50
☐	48515-8	FANTASY	$2.50
☐	48550-6	THE GODS LAUGHED	$2.95
☐	48579-4	GUARDIANS OF TIME	$2.95
☐	53567-7	HOKA! (with Gordon R. Dickson)	$2.75
	53568-5		Canada $3.25
☐	48582-4	LONG NIGHT	$2.95
☐	53079-9	A MIDSUMMER TEMPEST	$2.95
	53080-2		Canada $3.50
☐	48553-0	NEW AMERICA	$2.95
☐	48596-4	PSYCHOTECHNIC LEAGUE	$2.95
☐	48533-6	STARSHIP	$2.75
☐	53073-X	TALES OF THE FLYING MOUNTAINS	$2.95
	53074-8		Canada $3.50
☐	53076-4	TIME PATROLMAN	$2.95
	53077-2		Canada $3.50
☐	48561-1	TWILIGHT WORLD	$2.75
☐	53085-3	THE UNICORN TRADE	$2.95
	53086-1		Canada $3.50
☐	53081-0	PAST TIMES	$2.95
	53082-9		Canada $3.50

Buy them at your local bookstore or use this handy coupon:
Clip and mail this page with your order

TOR BOOKS—Reader Service Dept.
P.O. Box 690, Rockville Centre, N.Y. 11571

Please send me the book(s) I have checked above. I am enclosing
$_____ (please add $1.00 to cover postage and handling).
Send check or money order only—no cash or C.O.D.'s.

Mr./Mrs./Miss _____

Address _____

City _____ State/Zip _____

Please allow six weeks for delivery. Prices subject to change without
notice.